"M

"Huh?"

"Those bottles and chimes. Charms. You see them in different parts of the world. Some for the evil eye, some for good luck…"

"Love charms?"

He laughed softly. "Considering where we are, I'm betting on it."

She lifted her eyes to the jangling chimes, wary but curious. He wondered if she believed in them. He knew that luck was what you made it. And so was love. *Dammit,* he thought. *It's now or never.* Her face, still tilted toward the chimes, was open to him. He knew exactly what she would taste like seconds before his lips landed on hers. Red wine and mangoes. A warm sweetness all her own.

Immediately, her lips parted and softened, opening for him. When the tips of their tongues touched, he felt as if someone had tossed a transistor radio into his bathtub. The jolt was so sharp it almost singed his hair. He felt her sigh softly into his mouth.

He let one hand rise to cup her pointed chin, but was reminded of her injury by the roughness of the bandage.

"Sorry," he murmured, taking his hand away.

She grasped it and rested it lightly against her cheek, nestling into it.

Books by Simona Taylor

Kimani Romance

Dear Rita
Meet Me in Paris
Intimate Exposure
Everything to Me

SIMONA TAYLOR

lives on her native Caribbean island of Trinidad—a fertile place for dreaming up scorching, sun-drenched romance novels. She balances a career in public relations with a family of two small children and one very patient man, while feeding her obsession with writing.

She has also published three works of women's literary fiction under her real name, Roslyn Carrington, but it is her passion for romance that most consumes her. When not dreaming up drool-worthy heroes, she updates her website, www.scribble-scribble.com.

Everything to ME

SIMONA TAYLOR

KIMANI
ROMANCE
TM

Dedicated to my father, Trevor, and my grandparents,
Rosa, Vas and Fred. I miss you guys all the time.
I want to pick up the phone and call you every day,
but I can't. I want you all to know that I'm still writing.

Ros.

 KIMANI PRESS™

ISBN-13: 978-0-373-86263-4

EVERYTHING TO ME

Copyright © 2012 by Roslyn Carrington

Recycling programs
for this product may
not exist in your area.

www.kimanipress.com

Printed in U.S.A.

Dear Sister in Romance,

I hope you enjoy *Everything to Me.* This is the second novel I've set in Tobago, where my grandmother was born. We vacationed there every year, and I have many memories of my childhood there: sailing from Trinidad on a rickety overnight ferry—and once on my grandfather's tiny, open fishing boat, and watching crab and goat races on the beach. I'm always glad to share my pride and delight with you. Better yet, why not come see for yourself? I'll take you to this great place I know where we can eat right on the beach…

Even if you can't hop on a plane, pass by my website, www.scribble-scribble.com. There's always a breath of fresh Caribbean air waiting there for you. You can also reach me at roslyn@scribble-scribble.com, or on Facebook, Shelfari, or on my author pages at Harlequin.com or Amazon.

Keep reading!

Simona

Chapter 1

Trent Walker. On *her* plane.

Shoot me now.

Dakota Merrick sank a little deeper into the plush upholstery of her seat and watched as Walker sauntered up the aisle of the first class cabin. He held a leather laptop case in one hand, and a long, camel-colored coat was slung over his arm. He was casually dressed in a deep green polo and dark jeans and oh, yes, they both fit him quite nicely. The rich fabric clinging to him allowed her to make out the imprint of toned pecs and biceps.

Not that she was admiring them or anything.

As he drew closer, Dakota became aware of an itch rising somewhere in her midsection and creeping upward, like an invasion of teeny baby spiders. Up, up, over her chest and throat, up into her hair, and…oh, ugh. Spider metaphors were so uncool. She was a better writer than that.

He was even closer now. Damn.

It was a six-hour flight from the small eastern seaboard city of Santa Amata. If she'd been granted three wishes by a genie, she was pretty sure that being trapped for so long in a flying potato-chip can with the great Trent Walker wouldn't be one of them.

Especially since the last time they'd met, she'd almost got herself arrested.

He was not going to sit next to her. He was not… She'd rather sit next to a toddler with an ear infection. Anything would be better than being stuck with…

She was relieved to see that he was stopping two rows ahead. Dakota watched as he checked his ticket, his long face tilted down, his eyes hidden behind thin, expensive sunglasses. Then he lifted his head, verified his seat number and seemed satisfied.

Easily, he popped open the storage bin and stowed his haphazardly folded coat inside. He held on to the laptop. Sure he would, she thought. The music genius was probably going to work through the whole flight.

She looked down at the pile of magazines she'd brought with her, and tried not to feel competitive. There'd be more than enough work to keep her occupied once she got to Tobago, she reminded herself. She didn't need to get all workaholic up in here.

A chubby-legged young girl in a too-short denim skirt—which looked more like a wide, clingy belt than anything else—squeezed past Walker, looked up into his face with a pardon-me smile, and stopped dead. Dakota could hear the squeal of recognition from where she sat.

Trying not to roll her eyes, she watched the two briefly exchange words. Walker was smiling nonchalantly, while the girl quivered like an overexcited rabbit and flipped her purple-streaked hair. He reached into his laptop pocket, pulled out a small card, wrote something on it and extended it to her between two fingers. She clasped it to her chest like it was Willy Wonka's golden ticket, then did a little happy dance, chubby ankles tripping past each other in lace-up platform shoes.

Now Dakota really *did* roll her eyes.

Traffic in the aisle was backing up, so Walker excused himself with an incline of his head, and slid into his row. He smiled goodbye to the bunny rabbit and she jiggled down the aisle. She stopped, as luck would have it, right next to Dakota. Dakota rose and slid out, allowing her access to the window seat, glancing in Walker's direction as she did so.

She was startled to discover that he was looking in hers.

His expression could have won him a prize at a lemon-sucking contest. Slowly, one long hand came up and removed the glasses, as if he needed more light to determine if it really was her. With that gesture, he revealed eyes that reminded her of the buttered toffee she used to make candy apples with as a kid. But in those eyes… There was no warmth there. The unsmiling set of his full mouth immediately squelched that happy memory.

Okay, so Walker was as thrilled to see her as she was to see him.

His momma must have raised him right, though, because he acknowledged her with a polite—if stiff—dip of the head. She responded with a dip of her own, and then hastened to get back into her seat. By the time she finished fussing with her seat belt, he was sitting in the aisle seat, and all she could see was his hand and the back of his head as he popped in his earbuds. Seemed the man liked to listen to music while he worked. Not surprising, considering his whole life revolved around it.

"Do you know who that is?" the bunny squealed in her ear as she clicked her seat belt shut.

"I've got a pretty good idea," she answered dryly.

"That's Trent Walker. You know, like, Outlandish Music, Trent Walker? The owner?"

Dakota looked past her seatmate onto the tarmac. April rain slashed at the windows. She hoped it wouldn't delay their departure. Maybe if the engines started up, it would drown out the starstruck yipping. But if Walker's momma had raised him well, hers had raised her better, so she smiled and said, "Sure is. Not a face you can miss."

"Tell me about it! He's off da hook, ain't he? And I'm not just talking 'bout his *face*. He's hotter than half the acts he produces. And we're on the same plane. Can you believe it?" As the muted vibrations began humming through the cabin, her seatmate lifted her voice to be heard over the din. "And he's going to the Tobago Jazz Festival, just like me. You going?"

Dakota nodded. She was pretty sure everyone on the plane was headed to Jazz. It was one of the most popular annual music events in the Caribbean, and music lovers from all over the world were streaming in for it. Although Tobago was a mere speck of an island, home to only sixty thousand people, music legends like Whitney Houston, Elton John, Smokey Robinson and James Ingram had set the festival stages on fire in years gone by.

The girl waved the piece of paper she was clutching. "He just wrote me a backstage pass. I can go back after any show and talk to the stars. Big stars, girl. Giants!" She clasped her hands in elaborate prayer and looked heavenward. "Oh, please, let Erykha be there! That would be sooo… You want a backstage pass? You should get one." The girl prodded Dakota in the ribs. "Go 'head. Ask him. Fast, before we get airborne. Go on!"

The thought of her begging a favor off Trent Walker made her grin, but she explained gently, "Thanks, but I already have a pass. All access," she couldn't resist adding, and reprimanded herself for being childish.

"Really? What're you, like…." Large black eyes gave Dakota the once-over. "…a backup singer or something?"

Dakota wondered if she should be offended that the youngster hadn't pegged her for a main act. She shook her head. "Nope. Can't sing a note. It's a press pass. I'm a writer. A music columnist."

"Oh." The interest faded, what with Dakota not being a famous entertainer or anything. "Well, Trent Walker's got like, three acts performing at Jazz. Mango Mojo— the boy band, you know, with the sideburns guy? And Ryan Balthazar, and Shanique. She's out of rehab, did you hear? First time back on stage." She fluffed her purple-striped hair airily. "And I'm gonna get to meet them."

You'll meet them sooner than I will, Dakota thought, since Walker had shot down any hope of her ever interviewing his acts. The name Shanique tripped her up like a pothole on an otherwise smooth road. Yeah, she'd heard a little something about Shanique being out of rehab. Guiltily, her glance flew in Walker's direction—and found he was looking back, over his seat, his steady eyes reflecting nothing.

Her seatmate clapped her hand over her mouth. "OMG! He's looking at me!" She grabbed one of Dakota's magazines and hastily opened it, pretending to read. "Is he still staring?"

Yeah, Dakota thought. *But not at you.* Walker shifted forward again, just as the plane lifted its nose and rose into the sky.

"It's safe," she informed Walker's newfound groupie. "He's turned back around."

The girl clamped the magazine to her chest with a sigh. "Oh, man. Just think, a whole week in the hot Caribbean sun, rum parties all day, jazz all night, with dudes that look like him roaming around." The youthful face turned mischievous. "A week's a long time, and I'm sure he's gonna be hanging out backstage." She twirled the square of cardboard Walker had signed. "And something as fine-looking as that, you just gotta have a taste, ya know?" She flicked her tongue past her purple-painted lips, and Dakota tried not to be shocked, either by the suggestion or by the diamond that glinted at the tip of her tongue.

"How old are you?" she blurted.

"Old enough," the girl said, and laughed.

The first thing to hit Dakota was the scent of the island. Even as she stood just outside Crown Point International, with passengers bustling by and taxis honking, a sweet perfume asserted itself. It was a smell that made her think of melting brown sugar, suntan oil, fishing nets and pounding waves. She craned her head in the direction of a row of coconut trees, trying to catch a glimpse of the softly undulating water beyond. She felt like dropping her suitcase and handbag, kicking off her shoes, and running toward that wonderful surging surf.

Fortunately, good sense prevailed. This was *not* a vacation. She wasn't here to work on her tan or to snorkel. She was here to cover the jazz festival for her widely syndicated magazine entertainment column. That meant checking in at her hotel, getting some shut-eye and heading out to the main venue in the morning to start trawling for stories.

She held on tightly to the handle of her luggage, feeling a little ridiculous and overdressed in her close-fitting black leather skirt and knit top. They had kept her warm and dry on the other end of the trip, as foul weather prevailed on the East Coast. But here, in Tobago, even after six in the evening, cotton shorts and sandals would have been far more appropriate.

She turned her head, looking for her shuttle. Her assistant had booked her a suite in a hotel called the Sea Urchin, and they in turn had promised to send a ride for her when she landed. But she'd been waiting twenty minutes, and there was no sign of a vehicle with a blue-and-silver logo.

As she waited, Dakota idly took in her surroundings. The airport was tiny, a long building with a driveway running right through it, arrival and departure facilities on one side, and a series of small shops and booths on the other. Shop windows were jam-packed with tanning oils, brightly printed T-shirts, bikinis and sundresses. Women at vendors' tables, wearing bright floral aprons, yelled at passersby to sample their homemade peppermint sticks and coconut candies.

She fished out the notebook she'd jotted down the

hotel's particulars in and consulted it, then squinted at the signs and buildings nearby. She was in the correct spot, all right. There were other hotel cars around, and a press of taxi drivers in neat white shirts and black trousers, all clamoring for attention. Every now and then one would approach her, dark face split with a grin, and flash an ID badge. "Taxi?" She shook her head, and kept waiting.

Sea Urchin, Sea Urchin! Where are you?

Something rolled through her, tingly enough to be uncomfortable. She recognized it at once: a danger signal. She spun around, bringing her hand unconsciously to the back of her neck to smooth down the fine hairs that were at full attention. Trent Walker was strolling in her direction with that fine, easy walk of his, hips loose, long legs scissoring past each other. She had to consciously restart her heart.

They'd met five or six times, mainly at industry events. The last time she'd spoken with him, they'd been at a big album launch in Manhattan, he as a guest, she as a member of the media. It could have been seven months, easily, although the details of their encounter had the immediacy of a recent memory. His star artiste, the dark and glorious Shanique, had still been in rehab, recovering from a drug and alcohol habit, when she should have been on a Mediterranean tour that would have put millions into her pocket—and Walker's. And as for him, while his name wasn't exactly mud in an industry that had seen far worse sins than the one he'd committed, he wasn't exactly untouched by the scandal that ensued when Dakota's story hit the papers.

Walker acted like it was all Dakota's fault. But Dakota had simply broken the story of Shanique's drug abuse—and the lengths Walker had gone to cover it up. She'd been lucky, and had a connection who led her to the right source. She'd caught it and run with it. The story had doubled the number of papers in which her column appeared. Who could blame her?

Walker could, that's who.

He'd had a few choice words for her that night, and said things he shouldn't have about her character. She'd responded in a way that would have been funny in a cartoon, but wasn't appropriate in the middle of a cocktail party with the movers and shakers of the music world—not to mention the press—looking on.

She'd been a naughty girl.

He was coming closer still. *Disappear,* she willed herself, scrunching her eyes shut. She wished she could change color, like a tree frog or a chameleon, and blend in seamlessly with the background. Mutant style.

Unfortunately, she didn't have a mutant gene in her body. She opened her eyes and saw his head turn toward her…and then he was making his way through the crowd. Adrenaline surged. She had the urge to turn and run.

But she was glued to the ground, partly a victim of indecision, and partly mesmerized by the sight of him as he walked. Confident, easy, relaxed. He carried his bag with the laptop case strapped to it, not dragging them as she did, but dangling them effortlessly at the end of his arm. And triple dammit to hell, he looked fine.

Walker was as blessed with good looks as any one of his singers, and almost as sought after by the tabloids. Yet he seemed to have an uncanny knack for staying below their radar. Other than the occasional Page 5 photo of him on the red carpet with some arm candy, and the persistent rumors that he and the legendary Shanique had a thing going on, nobody had ever gotten close enough to him to publish much more. He liked to keep it that way; he'd refused to grant Dakota an interview more than once—and that was *before* she'd broken the story that had rocked his business.

"Miss Merrick." His tone was casual. Obviously, despite his reaction on the plane, seeing her hadn't rattled him half as much as *his* presence rattled *her*. Not that it *should* bother him. Music was her business, just as it was his. Surely he should have expected her to be there. Everybody who knew anything about music came to Jazz!

Two could play the cool game. "Mr. Walker," she replied smoothly. She turned and glared into the oncoming traffic.

He seemed to notice that all was not well with her world. "Problems?"

"You mean, apart from the fact that I've been standing here for half an hour waiting on my driver, and I don't see anyone with my hotel logo, or with my name on a sign?" The stress was evident in her voice.

He considered her for a while, his deep amber eyes examining her face until she became downright uncomfortable. Then he looked around. With a sweep of his arm, he indicated the airport fence and the road that lay beyond. "Maybe you should walk out to the curb. The crowd's a little thick in here. If you stand out there you might get a better idea of what's going on."

She looked in the direction he'd pointed. From what she could see through the chain-link fence, things didn't seem any less chaotic.

Next thing she knew, he had her suitcase in his other

hand and had already begun to walk, crossing the drop-off zone and moving past the shops. She snatched up her carry-on and ran after him, protesting. "I can carry my own bags!"

She might as well have been whistling in the wind.

Outside the main gates, he set their bags down. The concrete was sprinkled with a fine dusting of sand, crunching under her feet. She smelled that fragrance again, full of promise and invitation. She was too hungry and tired to answer its call. And after the cold, wet misery of her hometown, Santa Amata, the island heat was getting to her. *Please,* she prayed, *all I want is a shower, a meal and a good night's sleep.*

"I can take it from here," she told Walker, as politely but as firmly as possible.

"Hmm," he responded, but didn't move.

Suit yourself. She rummaged through her carry-on, found her phone, and poked at the numbers. Nothing. She tilted it so she could see the screen. Not a single measly bar. "Oh, just great." She glared at him as though the aura of magnetism surrounding him was responsible for the technical failure.

He reached into his pocket and withdrew his phone and held it out to her. "Try mine."

She gave it a suspicious look. Was it rigged to explode in her hand? "Why?"

He shrugged. "So you can get out of here, and I can go to my hotel with a clear conscience."

"Am I on your conscience?"

He paused for a moment before he answered. "Only to the extent that we're two American citizens landing on foreign soil, and one of us looks to be in trouble." Then he added, "Am *I* on *yours?*"

To save herself from answering, she grabbed his phone. It was smooth and warm to the touch. Naturally, it was the kind of gadget that could pick up a signal from Mars.

She dialed. On about the 20th ring, someone at the Sea Urchin got around to picking up. The conversation didn't last long.

"What do you mean, I'm not confirmed?" she blurted. "My assistant made that booking. Can you check again? Thank you. What? It's Merrick. M-e-double-r...but it has to be there." She realized she was squeezing the phone like a mamba with a rat. The voice on the other end was lilting and musical, but what it was saying was anything but gratifying.

"Can I make another booking, then?" She hated the sound of pleading in her tone, especially since Walker made no attempt to disguise the fact that he was listening. She nodded, groaned and clicked the phone off, teeth grinding.

"What's the problem?" he asked, as though he hadn't been overhearing every word.

"The problem is," she explained tautly, "that my new assistant forgot to confirm my booking. And with all the people turning up for the Jazz Festival, they haven't got any rooms. From what they're telling me, there's hardly a room left on the island."

He contemplated her predicament soberly. "What're you going to do?"

"Find another hotel," she said, as though it was the world's stupidest question. Hotel information wasn't going to fall from the sky; she'd have to find some help. Back at the airport, she remembered seeing a tourist bureau. She spun around and started dragging her suitcase.

To her surprise, he fell into step. She stopped so hard her shoes squeaked. "Where do you think you're going?"

"Walking you to wherever you're going for help."

Did music impresarios get merit badges for being nice to stranded travelers? "Why? I'm a grown woman."

Lazily, he let his eyes roam her body, something on his face telling her he was well aware she was a woman. "I told you—"

"I know," Dakota interrupted. "Two Americans on foreign soil, and all that. Thanks for being so patriotic, but if I really get into deep trouble, I'll take it to the embassy."

When he smiled, his long face, the same color as the sand scattered at their feet, almost warmed…but his voice held a note of amused mockery. "Our nearest embassy is one island over, in Trinidad."

"I'll be fine anyway," she said with dignity. "I can take care of myself."

His shapely lips tautened, and she knew exactly what was going through his head. "Yes, I forgot. You're very good at taking care of your own interests." Carefully, he set down her bag, hefted his, and stepped away. "Good luck. I imagine I'll be seeing you around at the festival?"

She shrugged. "I'm covering it, so I guess…"

"Well," he said, his voice dripping with irony. "I hope you find the stories you're looking for." His bag swung as he walked away.

Sure, you do, Dakota thought.

She didn't step into the tourist office until he was out of sight.

Chapter 2

Island time, Walker thought. No matter how often he traveled through the Caribbean, he never ceased to marvel at the slow, easy pace of everything and everyone around him. Coffee shop attendants stopped to chat in the middle of pouring him a cup, porters took their own sweet time crossing the road... Car rental companies moved with the speed of honey dripping off a spoon.

The previous client—no doubt an islander, he thought wryly—had returned the rental car he ordered more than an hour late, whereupon smiling employees had informed him in their musical accent that they'd clean the car up for him "just now." Suspecting that "just now" in island-speak meant a good chunk of time, he'd bought himself a local paper and settled in for the wait.

By the time they'd handed over the keys to the pearl gray BMW sedan, it was fully dark outside. He eased past the airport, noticing that traffic had thinned significantly. The flight they were on was probably the last international arrival of the evening. Everyone had already gone home.

At least, those who had a home to go to.

In the yellow glow of a streetlamp, a hunched shape sat on a bench, two small bags propped up beside her. Merrick, he knew at once. The curve of her shoulders, her mere presence, in fact, told him she hadn't found a place to sleep. He wondered idly how she planned on dealing with her assistant when she got back to New York. From his brief experiences, Merrick had quite a tongue on her; he was half-sorry for her assistant once Merrick could rustle up a few bars of signal on her phone.

As he rolled past, struggling to remember to drive on the left rather than the right, he turned his head—and their eyes locked. Hers were wide and dark against her tan skin, Japanese anime-huge, and in a flash he read anxiety and fear. One hand clutched the collar of her leather jacket to her throat. It was still warm out, so it couldn't have been to ward off the cold. In his rearview mirror, he saw her slap at her neck and wince.

In the darkness, the mosquitoes had come out.

The gods were having a laugh at her expense. Poetic justice, given the mess she'd almost made of his career.... Well, technically she'd made a mess of Shanique's career; he'd survived virtually unscathed. But still... Feeling guilty at the meanness of the thought, he comforted himself. She'd get lucky; it was mathematically impossible for every single bed on the island to be filled. She'd try again in a while, and at the very least find a dive where the all-night bar would keep her up and the bedbugs wouldn't give her a moment's rest.

Then maybe she'd be too tired in the morning to do any more muck-raking for her damn column.

In the rearview mirror, he saw the light above her head flicker, and she tilted her face upward in panic.

Walker eased his foot off the accelerator.

The woman was alone and possibly in danger. Who knew what kind of creatures, two-legged or otherwise, came crawling out of their holes after dark? What if something happened to her out there? A feeling of dread, mingled with a vague sense of responsibility, ran through him. If you saw someone standing on the tracks and a train was bearing down, only they couldn't hear it coming, would you push them out of the way?

Would you yank them out of harm's reach even if they'd done you wrong?

Naw, the voice in his head chided, *you're not thinking....*

With a squeal of tires, he made a U-turn, and headed back to where she sat. As he slammed on the brakes, her face was the picture of confusion and alarm.

"Get in, Merrick," he ordered.

"What?"

He hopped out, walked around, and grabbed her bags. "You can't stay here."

"I wouldn't be the first traveler to spend the night at an airport," she said stubbornly. "There's security all over the place. I'll be safe."

"It's a dinky country airport—an *open air* airport—on one of the smallest islands on the planet. And in case you haven't noticed, most everyone's gone home. What were you planning to do? Sleep on the bench?"

"I was planning to *stay awake* on the bench," she

countered, and slapped at the back of her neck again. "I hear the sun rises early in the West Indies."

"There are mosquitoes dancing around your head. Can you imagine what you'll look like by morning?"

"What's it to you?" she responded suspiciously.

"Refer to my previous statement about leaving fellow citizens stranded." He could have added a comment about damsels in distress, but he knew he'd be an idiot to go there. Merrick looked unlikely to be amused by his chivalry.

"I'll be sure the president's notified." She folded her arms, but didn't make a move.

As he threw her bags into the back, next to his, her dark eyes rounded. "What are you...?"

"Far as I know, my place is confirmed and waiting for me. You're welcome to come along."

She gasped. "Stay with you? In your room?"

He laughed, delighted by her horrified reaction. "Don't be ridiculous. I wasn't suggesting we share a bed...." He stopped, and his tongue flicked against his lower lip. "Not even one of those chaste little arrangements where one of us sleeps on top of the sheets and the other sleeps beneath them. This isn't a teen sitcom."

She looked relieved to hear it. "But how...?"

He explained. "I've rented a cabin. It's a fully equipped unit." Then he added meaningfully, "It has two *separate* bedrooms."

All the while he was talking, that self-preserving voice at the back of his head was calling him a lunatic. *Look at her,* the voice warned, *with her heart-shaped little face and pointed chin.* Plus, under that outfit—was she crazy, wearing leather *here?*—he knew she was more than a handful up top, and everything a brother could ask for down below.

Oh, yeah, he taunted himself. *You've noticed her over the months.* Just how small is this cabin, he wondered. Would he be able to stay out of her range?

He'd better.

She was frowning. Thinking. Tempted. She glanced at her stuff, sitting in the trunk of the Beemer. "I don't…"

He sighed; his patience was giving out. "It's late, Merrick. We've flown all day, and we're in a strange country. Stop fighting it. You need a meal and rest as much as I do. Come with me, just for tonight. You can call around for a hotel again in the morning."

"There'll be something for me tomorrow," she wavered.

"Definitely," he agreed, although he wasn't betting on it.

It was futile trying to resist the onslaught of logic. Slowly, doubtfully, she nodded. "We split the tab," she insisted.

"Deal." He patted her lightly on the shoulder, the first time he'd intentionally touched her. He felt something shift deep inside. "Let's go."

She climbed into his car like it was a paddy wagon carting her off to jail. As she buckled up, he noticed her hands were shaking. He wanted to say something to put her at ease, but for the life of him, he couldn't think of what.

He levered his long body into the driver's seat next to her and unfolded a small map, clicking on the overhead lights with one hand.

"Know where you're going?" Dakota asked.

He ran his finger along a fat blue line, tilting the map toward her so she could see as well. "It's fairly straightforward. Just got to stick to the coastal road 'til we get to Speyside."

"Is it far?"

Meaning how long would she be stuck with him, he thought. "The island's about 25 miles long. I don't expect anything's far from anything else." He gave her an amused look. "Don't worry about it. You don't even have to talk to me if you don't want to. Just lean back and listen to the music." He clicked on the radio and scrolled through the stations until he found one that suited him. Jazz, naturally.

"We'll be there in no time," he promised.

"Thank you," she murmured.

"My pleasure." The word *pleasure* rolled off his tongue.

Mistake, the voice in his head harped. *Big, big mistake.*

Dakota had the distinct impression Walker was driving with a lighter foot than he would have if he were alone. Even so, less than an hour later the car turned onto a narrow, sand-swept driveway and slowed to a halt. She stole a look out of the window, while trying not to be too obvious about it.

The property rolled over low foothills to the dark sea. Moonlight glittered on the surface, breaking into a dozen pieces with the movement of the waves, until each piece danced to its own rhythm.

The softly lit estate was lined with greenery. She could just make out the silhouettes of tall, curving coconut trees that arched toward the sky, flanked by shorter, fan-shaped palms.

He helped her out, then yanked their bags from the trunk, holding one in each hand. "Come," was all he said.

She followed him, clutching her carry-on. In the back of her head, a mantra had struck up: *bad idea, bad idea, bad idea....* She shouldn't have let him talk her into this. She should have made a few more calls. Tried more hotels...

Beyond the trees, a pair of spotlights illuminated an arched gateway of wrought iron, shaped like rambling vines curling and intertwining around each other. The word Rapture spanned the two supporting posts.

Dakota stopped short. "Tell me that's not the name of the hotel!"

"I believe that's the name of the hotel." He seemed to be enjoying the shock in her voice. "Relax. It's an adults-only resort. They're all over the Caribbean: Hedonism, Sandals... It can't be much different."

"But why'd you pick this one?" she asked suspiciously. Maybe he was planning to take full advantage of all the delights available to a man of his stature at a festival like Jazz. She thought of the dizzy little groupie on the plane, with her diamond-studded tongue. Was Walker the kind of guy to choose the best of what was on offer at a concert and head back to his hotel to continue the party in private?

"By the time my assistant got around to booking, I didn't have much to choose from. My travel agent said they had an opening, and I took it." Then he reminded her, "It's better than your alternative, correct?"

She conceded both his point and her rudeness. "Sorry. I'm very grateful—"

He cut her off. "So relax and enjoy it." As he continued toward the entrance, his back turned to her, she heard him add, "You don't have to swim in the nude pool if you don't want to."

"What?" she gasped, but all she got in reply was a soft, throaty chuckle.

At the end of a stone walkway they came upon a brightly lit building. Its doors were open, and the entrance was flanked by tall torches, their ends rammed into the ground. The air was filled with the scent of citronella.

As Walker began to climb the four or five steps leading to the entrance, Dakota lagged behind, overwhelmed by growing panic.

He sensed her reluctance and stopped abruptly, turning slightly to look back at her. Since he didn't signal he was slowing down, she almost ran into him. His amusement at her discomfiture was all gone. He was just one step above, looking down into her face, his eyes searching hers for something. Maybe he found it, because he said, very gently, "Don't worry."

Instead of shooting back a skeptical response, she wet her lips and looked away. Nights were short on the islands, and things would look better in the morning. Plus, they weren't exactly *enemies;* it wasn't as if he'd sworn a blood oath to erase her and her kin from the earth. His business and her duty just weren't in sync. It wasn't personal.

Well, all right, it was a *little* personal. Like that evening at the album launch when he'd called her a bottom-feeding scavenger for ratting out his precious diva—*and him*. And she'd responded by decorating the front of his white shirt with a glass of '03 Chilean red.

A movement in the doorway saved her from whatever he was going to say next. The apparition was enough to jolt all thoughts of Walker from her mind, and that was saying something.

The man standing in the glowing lamplight at the entrance was so tall that he dwarfed Walker, and his skin was so black he seemed to belong to the night, rather than simply inhabit it. Impeccably twisted dreadlocks cascaded from his head, a Medusa's nest of snakes. He wore a tan suit made of a light fabric, with a cream-colored shirt and a tie of deep garnet. He was so striking, so physically perfect, that Dakota almost believed he was supernatural. This *was* the Caribbean, after all. A place populated by the ghosts of African princes, forest deities and enchanted apparitions.

As they approached, onyx eyes gleamed behind thin glasses, and his dark face split in a welcoming smile. His large, perfect teeth all but glowed. "Mr. Walker! So good to meet you. Welcome to Tobago." His deep voice floated on the wave of the graceful and enchanting accent they'd heard everywhere since they'd touched down.

Walker and the handsome devil clasped hands warmly, equally white grins on their faces. "Trent, please. And it's good to be here."

The big man turned his cave-dark eyes in Dakota's direction. His grin grew even wider. "I wasn't aware you were bringing a guest, Trent, but we're perfectly happy to have her." Then he addressed Dakota directly. "Welcome. I'm Dr. Declan Hayes, part owner of this establishment. But once you check in, there's a penalty for using last names here at Rapture." He cocked his head in the direction of the reception area. "We've got a clay jar in there, sort of like your American swear jar. If you call me Dr. Anything, you owe me a dollar. Deal?"

She couldn't help but smile. "Deal…Declan." She threw a glance at Walker. Damned if she was calling *him* by his first name. She'd drop a buck in Declan's jar every twenty minutes, if she had to.

Walker laughed, as if he knew what she was thinking. Then, realizing the introductions had been one-sided, said, "Declan, forgive my rudeness. This is Dakota Merrick. My…er…" He searched for several long seconds for a suitable description, and then finished up weakly "…colleague."

Declan caught his hesitation—and misunderstood. He lowered his voice, his face somber, radiating trustworthiness. "Don't worry, Trent, Dakota, here at Rapture, we're extremely discreet. Rapture was built for lovers, and confidentiality is our top priority. We have a wide range of indulgences to offer, and I promise you you'll be very happy together here."

Dakota choked on a mouthful of shock. "But I…but we…we're not…" She shot Walker an exasperated look.

Declan had already snatched up Dakota's bag and was moving. "Follow me to your quarters. You were lucky enough to get one of the largest and most luxurious cabins. It's the farthest from the communal areas, for enhanced privacy." He twinkled back at Dakota. "And the outdoor Jacuzzi tub is completely screened off from the other cabins."

Jacuzzi, Dakota huffed to herself. Adults only, built for lovers…

The two men fell into step, as though they were

old friends. Dakota kept up with them, seething. She wanted to grab this sleek gorgeous apparition, spin him around and make it abundantly clear that she and Trent Walker were not, not, not here for an illicit liaison. It was an accident they were even together.

They passed through a side door and descended a few steps into a garden that Dakota could only describe as magical. Even through the thick soles of her shoes she could feel the springiness of the dense, spiky grass. Under soft outdoor lights, a chaotic array of bushes, flowers and trees slumbered. Flagstone paths twisted and twined, going off into arbitrary directions. Down each path, she could see a faint halo of light, leading her to believe that each one led to a cabin.

"The pool's in that direction," Declan volunteered.

The nude pool, she remembered.

"It's right next to the spa, where you can enjoy a variety of services: hot-cupping, Swedish massage, Shiatsu, acupressure. My business partner, Anke, is in charge of that. My office is on the other end of the property, if you'd like to have an appointment."

She just had to ask. "Appointment? For...?"

"Counseling. I started off as a general medical practitioner, but then went back to study psychiatry. Now I'm a sex and relationship therapist," Declan answered calmly.

Sex and relationship therapist. Huh. She distracted herself from the incongruity of the situation by focusing on her surroundings. She wished desperately that it was still daylight so she could enjoy the sights as well as the smells. What a long way from Santa Amata, with its endless rain and slush. She was in the warm and wonderful Caribbean, so close to the sea she could hear it whisper in and whoosh out. The sky was so bright and clear she wanted to reach up, snatch down stars and make herself a sparkling necklace.

She didn't realize she was smiling until she heard Walker murmur, "I know. Makes you tingle all over, doesn't it?"

The last thing she wanted to discuss with Walker was any part of her body tingling. With a nervous hand, she twisted a curly lock of hair around her ear.

The path dipped sharply and they came upon an exquisite cabin. It was made of wood and painted a mellow tangerine, except for the carved white adornments that graced the small porch, doors and windows, and ran around the edge of the roofing like spider webs.

Wood thudded dully under their feet as they climbed the three steps leading to the entrance. Declan withdrew a key from his pocket, and slid it into the lock. He eased the door open and preceded them into the cabin, flicking on lights as he did so.

He led them through the sitting area toward the farthest bedroom and flooded it with light. Its walls were a soothing shade of avocado set off by white jalousies. A large painting hung on one wall, an oil rendition of a dark-skinned woman, completely naked, rising out of a tropical stream, water dripping from her long, woolly hair. Water rose just to her pubis, seeming to caress her there, like a cool, intimate hand. The thick-lashed, heavy-lidded eyes were half closed, and her smile spoke of the pleasures of swimming naked. It was the most erotic painting Dakota had ever seen. She tore her eyes away.

She was vaguely aware of the other furniture. The

rest of her mind was swamped by the image of the big, luxurious bed.

"This is the master bedroom...." Declan was saying.

The king-size bed was covered with a cheerful quilt. It was strewn with huge pillows and stood high off the floor.

"Bathroom's over there," he continued.

The bed stood firmly on polished brass legs. The mattress was thick. Bouncy, she guessed. Strong. She caught sight of what was on the bedside table. Other hotels kept a copy of the Bible next to the bed. Rapture had a leather-bound copy of the *Kama Sutra.* She rolled her eyes.

"I'm sure you two will be very comfortable here." Declan set Dakota's bag down against a wall.

She sputtered, trying to drag her gaze—and her thoughts—away from that big, big bed and the ancient Indian instruction manual lying beside it. "Oh, but we…"

Walker still held on to his bag. Unruffled by the insinuation, he said calmly, "Dakota can take this one."

Her ears pricked up at his use of her first name. Just to avoid tossing a buck into Declan's jar?

He continued. "I'll be fine in the room next door." He cocked his head at her, as though amused by her discomfort, and gave her half a wink.

Declan's bushy brows flicked upward for a fraction of a second and then, with a nod toward Dakota, he followed Walker. She stood with her back to the door, surveying the room, thoughts tumbling.

Chapter 3

The men exchanged muffled goodbyes and there was the sound of the front door closing. Then, a presence in the doorway. She spun around.

Trent stood just a few feet before her, hands on hips, contemplating. The forced intimacy of shared quarters made it hard for her to breathe.

"Traveling's a real bitch," he finally said, sounding sympathetic. "You must be tired."

She was way too keyed up to be tired. "I'm…fine, thank you." She was carefully polite: as tense as the situation was, she couldn't forget she was here due only to his kindness.

"Good. Why don't we take twenty to freshen up? Then we can head out to the dining room and see what they're offering."

Eat. With him?

Her hesitation was just shy of being damn rude.

"Hey," he said reasonably, with that same easy smile that made him as much of a star as his singers, "if the Pilgrims and the Indians could call a truce long enough to eat…"

She could have countered with a sharp rejoinder about smallpox-infected blankets, but good manners forced her simply to nod in mute, weary gratitude.

He accepted her concession with the satisfaction of a man used to winning. "Twenty minutes, then." He headed back to his room.

"Anything you don't eat?" Trent asked as he studied the menu. All around them, guests were already dining in the gorgeously decorated hall. The meals were included in the price of the stay, so most of the hotel guests stayed on the grounds for dinner. The vaulted ceiling was bright white, and the glow from small lamps on each table danced along its surface like a light show.

Dakota sat in the comfortable polished teak chair, several degrees cooler now that she'd showered and changed into a light linen sleeveless dress with a square-cut neckline. She could have sworn for a second that, upon first seeing her, Trent's eyes had lingered briefly at her bare collarbone before sliding downward and away, but she could be mistaken.

The air was filled with the dizzying scent of hot food, an opulent blend of roasted meats, baked yams and potatoes, and vegetables drizzled with olive oil. A sharp pang of hunger stabbed at her, reminding her it had been hours since she'd had anything.

"I'm not normally fussy, but I hope the soup of the day isn't goat liver or something weird like that." She was startled to find her sense of humor hadn't abandoned her.

In response, the rigid squareness of his shoulders softened a little, letting her know she wasn't the only one anxious over their arrangements. "Well, they cater to Americans and Europeans, so I'm sure they'll have something less exotic for the guests. And I think that soup you're talking about is called mannish water. It's Jamaican, not Tobagonian."

"Well, if I ever go there, I'm not having any." She ran her finger around the top of her water glass, glad for something to focus on. Anything to keep her eyes off him.

"Where's your sense of adventure?" He seemed as relieved as she was to have something safe to talk about. As if food could be a safe topic in a place like Rapture. From what she'd seen so far, she'd be grateful if the coconut mousse wasn't molded in the shape of a penis.

As for her sense of adventure? She was having dinner in the least likely of places with the least likely of people. This was enough adventure for her.

At the next table, a movement caught her eye. A long-haired young man with deep blue eyes reached across the table to his companion, a champagne flute in his hand, and slowly drew the chilled glass over her left nipple. The woman laughed, and her physical reaction to the icy contact was instantly obvious as the small, hardened bump poked through the thin satin of her blouse. That simple gesture was so outrageously erotic that Dakota sucked in a lungful of air, shocked at herself for watching.

She exhaled through pursed lips, commanding her

body to be still. Many dangers lurked in this place. *One night,* she reminded herself. *It's just for one night.*

She could tell Trent was studying her reaction. The low light made long feathery shadows of his lashes. She noticed for the first time that a tiny mole perched near the corner of his lower lip. On a woman, it would have been a beauty mark. On a man, it was…something else. His smile was lazy, his gaze assessing. "I've never met a reporter who was a prude," he remarked.

"I'm a columnist, not a reporter," she answered, dragging her gaze away from the most erotic sight she'd seen in a long time. Upon deeper thought, it would have been a very long time since she'd even experienced something so erotic.

"I stand corrected." He tilted his head in the direction of the couple, who were about five minutes from getting it on right there at the table. "This really bothers you." It was a statement, not a question.

"No, it doesn't," she lied, and felt her face flush. "I'm not opposed to PDA, per se," she added, hating the primness in her voice.

"Just in my presence?"

"Don't flatter yourself."

A waitress arrived just in time to save her from his response. Trent asked the waitress to surprise them with their meals, which shocked the hell out of Dakota.

"Adventure," she noted dryly.

"I embrace it whenever it presents itself," he shot back smartly. Then his brow furrowed a bit. "Although maybe I should stop short of ordering red wine with the meal?"

She knew at once what he was referring to: her wine-pouring escapade at the cocktail party seven months

ago. He'd deserved it, she reminded herself, for his behavior. Rather than be embarrassed, she felt a grin break
out. "I think your odds are good tonight."

"They'd better be. Don't want to lose another shirt."

"I sent you a replacement. Didn't it fit?"

"Perfectly," he conceded. "You have a very good
eye."

A clear implication that she'd been looking at him
long and hard enough to correctly guess his size. She
debunked that at once. "It was a wild guess."

He gracefully let the matter drop, and they settled
on cashew wine. The waitress floated away, promising
them she'd be back with their dinner "just now." At that,
Trent's lip twitched.

"What?"

"Nothing, but maybe you ought to fill in the cracks
with a few breadsticks while we wait."

She'd heard enough about island service to think that
was a good idea. As she broke off a crumbly piece of
bread and slipped it into her mouth, she hoped they'd
be too busy nibbling to make much small talk. No such
luck.

"What're your plans for tomorrow?" he asked.

"Find a hotel," popped out of her before she could
restrain it.

"I'm sure that'll be a priority," he agreed. "I meant,
apart from that."

"Oh," she said with deliberate casualness. "I think
I'll go down to the festival site and get started on my
interviews."

He tautened visibly, but his voice was steady. "Do
you already have appointments booked?"

"Of course, a few," she said noncommittally, and

couldn't stop herself from adding, "but none with your people."

He smiled like a wolf. "Did they all turn you down? Even Mango Mojo? Those youngsters would grant an interview with a supermarket rag if they thought it would give them more exposure."

The comparison between her nationally syndicated column and a write-up in a tabloid stung like blazes. She worked hard on her craft and was well respected in many entertainment circles for her writing. The fact that Trent seemed stubbornly intent on not acknowledging her successes rankled. But instead of defending her work, she retorted, "Yeah, they all turned down my requests. And why wouldn't they? You obviously told them to avoid me like I've got leprosy."

His face didn't even twitch. "I gave no such instruction."

"Oh, don't ask me to believe—"

"I'm their producer, not their publicist. I don't decide who they talk to and who they don't—"

"But you must have let on how you feel about me," she argued.

He shrugged. "I've never made my feelings a secret. Anyone who knows anything about the industry knows what went down last year, and what happened after your column hit the newsstands."

What went down last year…as if she needed a reminder. Shanique was enjoying a meteoric rise up music's A-list, was on the second album of a four-disc deal with Trent's Outlandish Music and had celebrity endorsements piled up to her impressively sculpted butt. Those who'd noted a few cracks appearing in her stunning facade had chosen to overlook the growing problems. There was talk of her losing her voice, her edge. She'd denied it, claiming that her album and concert sales were proof enough that she was still on top of her game. Until Dakota's story broke that instead of singing live at her sold-out concerts, Shanique, due to her overindulgent drug use, had been lip-synching to the voice of another singer, hidden backstage.

Dakota's solid connection with the right person... She stopped midthought. Truth be told, she could hardly call her source *the right person,* considering how much pain he'd caused her. Deliberately, carefully, she rephrased, even if it was only inside her head. Her solid, *well-connected source* had gotten her the exclusive and all the proof the doubters needed. It was the exposé of Dakota's career. Shanique had denied it until she was purple, sobbing to anyone who would listen that she'd been set up, and the whole thing was a ruse to make her look bad. While some of her fans took it in stride— stuff like that did happen in the music business, after all—others were outraged at spending their hard-earned money on tickets to hear someone else sing. Websites and Facebook pages sprang up overnight, boycotting her concerts and demanding their ticket money back. Parodies of her fraudulent performance went viral on YouTube. The sponsors took notice. Endorsement deals dried up like a creek in Death Valley.

Trent's reputation also took a hit. Questions rolled in. As Shanique's producer—and rumored lover—had he known about her subterfuge? Did he willfully aid and abet? Had it been his idea all along? His publicist had released a statement expressing concern for Shanique's well-being, while stopping short of admitting any involvement in the lip-synching debacle. Nonetheless, the damage was done.

Their waitress arrived with steaming bowls of dark green soup, just in time to stop Dakota from getting further sucked into the depths of Trent's accusing gaze. He seemed glad for the distraction. "Callaloo soup," he informed her, reading off a small card that came with the meal. "It's like spinach."

She'd have eaten warmed-up tar if it meant they could change the subject. She sipped experimentally and discovered it was pretty good.

That could have put an end to the conversation, but the man had a one-track mind. "I never banned them from giving you an interview, Dakota."

There: he was using her name again. She swallowed a mouthful of hot liquid. "But they won't."

He shrugged eloquently.

"And neither will you," she couldn't resist pointing out.

"Did you expect me to?" The thought seemed to amuse him.

"Not since…my story, sure. I understand that. But you turned me down well before—"

"I'm not very good with the media," he responded offhandedly.

"Then you're in the wrong field."

He gave her a slow smile, one that had a curious effect on her stomach. "Oh, I'm pretty sure I'm in the right field. Music is my life, and my life is music. I'm just lucky I can afford to hire people to handle stuff I'd rather not do."

"Such as interviews with bottom-feeding scavengers like myself." She quoted one of the last things he'd said to her at the cocktail party months ago. Even to her own ears, she still sounded hurt.

He must have heard it, too, because he leaned forward, and his self-satisfied smile faded. "I apologize if my words were a little…harsh. I'm not normally that uncouth. I was a bit ruffled at the time."

He had been ruffled? Just thinking about the way he'd repeatedly dismissed her made her feathers curl. "You're prejudiced," she told him bluntly.

He looked shocked. "Excuse me?"

"You don't know who I am or what I'm capable of. You treat me like I'm nothing more than a tabloid hack—"

"Your story on Shanique had all the hallmarks of a hack job—"

"It did not," she defended herself hotly. She counted her points off on her fingers. "It was well researched, well substantiated and it turned out to be one hundred percent true. And yet you made a decision about me, and that's the end of that," Dakota said with finality. "You call yourself a businessman, but you don't have the guts to change your mind once it's made up. I'd have thought someone in your position would be more flexible."

She went on, too upset to care if she was treading on his toes. "And furthermore, all you care about is how my column affected you and your precious goldmine. But Shanique needed to be reined in and helped, and nobody around her, none of you who knew her, did anything about it. I know that these days, the music business is more about image than substance—"

"Shanique has true talent," he interrupted at once. "She has perfect pitch. Her vocal range spans almost four octaves."

"It certainly didn't last year," Dakota shot back. "Or she wouldn't have had to get help from an out-of-work R&B singer called Michelle." She was surprised at how upset she was getting at his instinctive defense of his superstar. She slapped her hand on the table to make her point. "Shanique's fans didn't deserve to be cheated out of their hard-earned money. What she did to her fans and to her body was wrong, and somebody had to say something."

"And secure their own writing career while they're at it," he countered scornfully.

She ignored the assault on her motives. "I know I did the right thing. Did you?"

From the way he flinched, she could tell her barb had struck a nerve. She pressed home her advantage. "Not only that, but you compounded the appearance of guilt by saying precious little. You've consistently glossed over every single question aimed at you about the whole affair."

"I believe it's my constitutional right to—"

"Oh, please," she scoffed. "You know the music business better than that. If there's a void in information, people will fill it with whatever suits their fancy. Not facing it head-on only makes you look worse."

"Worse?"

"That you were complicit in the drug use. That you were a party to—or even the mastermind behind—the whole lip-synching scam."

"Operational issues such as her concert performances are the responsibility of her manager, not her producer," he protested.

"You work closely with all your acts. You had to have known."

His light skin took on a mottled hue; he was mighty irritated but struggling to hide it. *Take that,* she thought.

The waitress glided back into view, whisked away their soup bowls, and set down aromatic, steaming dishes. Like their appetizer, the meal came with a little menu card, which listed the featured food: spit-roasted chicken, herbed grouper and tomatoes stuffed with saffron rice. Glasses of amber-colored cashew wine were placed next to each plate.

When Dakota lifted her glass, her hand shook slightly. "Cheers," she said, clinging to her cool.

"The same." He lifted his glass to her.

Silence followed as they ate. Then, halfway through their meal, "Go ahead. Shoot."

She frowned. "What?"

"You wanted to interview me? Ask me a question."

Her little potshots had worked? Seriously? A man's ego really was his weakness. She looked around, flustered. "But I haven't prepared. I need notes…a recorder…"

"I'll bet you have an excellent memory."

She did, but still… "Here? Now?"

"Now or never." He was challenging her, testing to see what she was made of.

But her triumph had fizzled. He'd thrown her off balance with his acquiescence, and all she could manage was a weak, "How old are you?"

"Thirty-four, but everybody knows that. That all you got?" His toffee-colored eyes were taunting.

She wished she had a paper napkin, anything to scribble a few notes on. What she really needed was a minute to clear her head. "What made you get into the music business?"

He opened his hands in an expansive gesture. "Are you writing for the school paper?"

He was right; she was handling this like a cub reporter. She bought herself a moment by taking a bite of the delicious chicken, asking herself what it was about him that so unnerved her. She was a writer, and a good one, and had done interviews with subjects far tougher than he. She needed to find her mettle.

She set her knife and fork down, straightened her spine, and nailed him to his chair with a look. "Mr. Walker," she demanded, "Did you have anything to do with Shanique's lip-synching scandal? When she stopped singing live at her concerts, and started using a voice double…when she started cheating her fans… did you know?"

He set down his cutlery as well, finished his cashew wine, and steepled his fingers. "You used my last name, you know. You owe Declan a buck."

She reached into her bag, extracted a dollar between two fingers, and laid it on the table before him. "Toss it into the jar next time you pass. Now answer the question."

He sighed heavily. "I knew. I was dead set against it. When Shanique's voice started to go, because of the…" He paused.

"Drug abuse," she added helpfully.

He nodded. "I considered canceling the last few concerts. She almost lost her mind…and so did the backers. My financiers."

"You'd have lost millions."

"Correct."

"So you decided the show had to go on."

"As I said, I didn't decide. The music director, her

voice coach and other…interested parties…thought it would be best for all involved. Shanique just had a few more shows to go before her tour ended, and then she could get some rest. And some…"

"Help."

"Correct," he said tautly.

She took one more step onto dangerous ground, and behind her, the path to safety faded in the distance. "Did you know she was using?"

The answer was curt. "I knew."

"And you did nothing?"

His expression darkened. "I know you don't think much of me, but no, not even a dipstick like me would sit by and watch a woman destroy herself. I tried talking to her. I scheduled appointments with a therapist. She missed all of them. I was setting things in place for an intervention when…" A disgusted *huff* escaped his clenched teeth. "When your unnamed *friend* slipped you the details of this story. And the rest, as they say…" He trailed off.

The wine went sour in her mouth. When her column first hit, she'd received a furious call from Trent himself, demanding that she tell him how she'd gotten her hands on the information, but she'd remained professionally silent. She followed the first rule of journalism: protect your source. And in her case, she had more than one good reason to do so. She wondered what he'd say if he only knew exactly who that friend was.

She couldn't…could *not* look at him. Her gaze dropped to her plate, and she discovered that the sight and smell of the meal she'd been enjoying so much had become overpowering. Her stomach rolled.

"Shanique made her own choices," Dakota reminded

him. "When you look at the bare bones of the case, she only has herself to blame."

"She did make her own choices," Trent agreed softly, much to her surprise. "Bad ones."

Dakota couldn't help but notice the tenderness with which Trent spoke of Shanique and her problem. Realization dawned. "It was you who made her go into rehab after…you know."

He nodded.

A memory resurfaced of Shanique outside the doors of an expensive rehab clinic, flashbulbs popping, a forest of microphones in her face as the newshounds, having caught wind of her presence, had converged on the scene. Tearfully apologizing for her actions, begging her fans to forgive her, promising she'd be back on stage once she was clean again. Trent had stood stoically by her side, his face a mask, eyes hidden behind dark glasses. One arm around her shoulders, the other urging the media back when they got too close. He was a silent, solid rock.

His protective body language, the way he positioned himself between Shanique and the aggressive slew of reporters, had spoken volumes. Only a man who loved a woman took that stance. Even as she asked the question, she knew there was no way he could deny it.

"You and Shanique really are romantically involved."

He looked directly into her eyes. "Are we involved? No."

She gasped. He was lying to her face! "How can you sit there and deny—"

"I'm not denying," he said crisply. "I'm being precise. Shanique and I aren't *romantically involved,* as you so delicately put it. Not now. We were. Past tense."

She tried to conceal her satisfaction, tried to put a lid on her rising excitement, but it was difficult. To her knowledge, Trent Walker had never publicly discussed his personal relationship with his biggest star, and here he was, admitting it to her. The next question was obvious. "What happened?"

"Rehab happened. Shanique's career taking a nosedive happened."

So the relationship had fallen apart in tandem with Shanique's career. His glittering singing star had gone supernova, and he'd bailed. Trent must have blamed Dakota for both catastrophes.

"You…broke up with her when she went into rehab."

His brows shot up, shock resonating in his voice. "*I…?* You must really think I'm a son of a bitch, huh?"

She was too confused by the passion in his response to speak.

She didn't have to. He continued, his words like acid rain. "I would never abandon a woman at the darkest point of her life. As much as it would surprise you, *she* broke up with *me*." The mole at the corner of his mouth was like a period at the end of an abrupt sentence.

He sat back, his rigid body going limp, the eyes that held hers losing focus as he gazed off into mid-distance. To Dakota's horror, a cloud of hurt and sadness drifted across his face. She was looking at a man who'd been burned, and who was tasting grief and rejection warmed over.

Then she understood. Dakota's story had led to Shanique's humiliation, which, in turn, had caused Shanique to push Trent away. No wonder Trent hated her.

To ask was to bring fire raining down onto her head, but she did so anyway. "Are you still in love with her?"

The warm eyes went cold. His chair scraped as he got abruptly to his feet. "Interview's over, Merrick," he told her.

He threw a dollar onto the table.

Chapter 4

There was a certain quality about Tobago that soothed Dakota. Everything moved in slow motion. People didn't rush; they ambled. They didn't yell; they sang their words. Nonchalant groups of men sat outside bars playing cards and drinking beer in the sunshine, and herds of goats and shorthaired sheep roamed untended along the beaches. A seductive peace permeated her bones, even though she was here to work…and was sitting beside a man who should still be pissed off at her after last night, but who was instead cordial and calm.

By the time she'd returned to the cabin—and, yeah, she'd dragged her feet a little—his bedroom door had been closed and there was no light shining from beneath. She'd spent the night marooned atop the huge brass bed in the master bedroom, listening for signs of activity in the next room, finally falling into a tense, exhausted sleep.

Although he'd politely offered to wait while she had breakfast, pointing out that he rarely had more than a cup of coffee himself, she'd rather go hungry than inconvenience him more than she already had. She'd grabbed a cup of locally grown coffee, pocketed an orange and a banana, and dragged her suitcase out to his car, a pointed reminder that after her day at the concert site, she was seeking her own accommodations.

As Trent drove, her entire body was aware of him next to her. She'd dreaded being stuck in the car with him, almost as anxious as the night before when she'd accepted his offer of a place to stay. Though he seemed more moodily introspective than angry, the pool of silence between them made her uncomfortable.

She filled the silence with babble, commenting on everything she saw including how tall the coconut trees were, how colorful the little houses, and how salty the sea breeze. She marveled at the bright piles of fruit sold at the side of the road by old women or young children. Trent responded to her conversational efforts, but didn't seem willing to start any of his own.

In the glare of the morning sun, she could see that the capital city, Scarborough, was an odd blend of old and new, with British forts and cannons as the backdrop for American fast-food joints and cybercafes. And the sea. The sea was everywhere. No matter which direction they turned, she could smell, see or hear it. Locals and tourists alike walked aimlessly along the roadside, towels tossed nonchalantly over their shoulders, swinging cotton totes filled with necessities.

At a traffic light, a dark, hulking man, with his thick dreads bleached orange by the salt water, thrust a live lobster at her. She shrieked. Trent declined the offer to buy, and as he peeled away from the light, Dakota caught a glimpse of the lobster, waving its banded claws goodbye—or beckoning for help.

With two days to the start of the festival, Immortelle Park was a beehive. Trucks and cars were parked haphazardly for a hundred yards, workers moving in equipment, designers erecting banners, decorations and signage. Sound people unrolled cables and yelled at each other. They were forced to park some distance away, even though Trent's rental sported a temporary VIP pass.

"Here we are," he said unnecessarily. He hopped out, walked around and opened the door for her.

She passed her hand through her hair. They each had work to do. He'd go off to see about his performers' affairs, and she'd start poking around for stories and keeping the appointments she'd made. "Um, well, thank you."

He regarded her quizzically. "For…?"

"For giving me a place to stay last night. You didn't have to do that."

He dismissed the thought with a gesture. "Anyone would have."

Not anyone. She wasn't sure she'd have been as noble if she'd been in his position. She pressed on anyhow. "Well, I was in touch with my assistant this morning."

"So your phone decided to give you a break?"

"I gave it a very stern talking to."

The twitch of a smile around his mouth surprised her. "And does your assistant still have a job?"

She couldn't stop her wry laugh. "For the time being. She got me a place she found on the internet. It's just outside Scarborough, so I'll be going over there when

I'm done here." She fished a bit of notepaper out of her bag and waved it at him as proof. "The Sugar Apple Inn, and I *am* confirmed this time."

"Sounds quaint."

By *quaint,* she guessed, he meant *basic.* She'd thought so, too. "So long as the bed's clean and dry," she said with a shrug. "I'm not picky."

"Glad you got that sorted out. I'm sure you'll be more comfortable on your own."

His unspoken words, *far away from me,* rang loud and clear. She glanced at the trunk. "If I can just have my bags…?"

He cocked his head to one side. "Where're you going to store them? How are you getting to the hotel?"

"I'll call a cab. The bags aren't that heavy. I could probably…" She trailed off. Probably what? Drag them behind her from interview to interview?

He pointed the key fob at the car and locked the doors with a decisive click. "Don't be ridiculous. Your bags are safe here. I'll drive you over when you're ready."

She opened her mouth to protest, and then common sense made her shut it again. He was right. They weren't in Santa Amata. Hailing a cab wouldn't be the easiest of tasks. She accepted his offer with grace. "Thank you."

"No problem." With a sweep of his arm, he invited her to walk with him. They picked their way through the crowd of workers, ducking to avoid two men carrying a sheet of plyboard on their shoulders. Near the entrance, a huddle of six or eight young boys gaped at the goings-on, enthralled by the excitement. They were dressed in ragged shorts, most of them barefoot and shirtless. A few of them clutched jam jars with small brown fish, obviously the bounty from a fishing expedition in a nearby stream.

As they passed the boys, the youngest, who couldn't have been more than four or so, waved at Dakota. He had a single, cheeky dimple. As she lifted her hand to wave back, a bull-necked man in a security guard's uniform charged out of the gate, yelling and cursing. The boys scampered off, laughing, the water sloshing out of the jars, imperiling the fish.

Dakota watched in astonishment as the man continued to hurl a barrage of obscene language at the kids. He waved his arms, threatening them with dire consequences if they came back to his park. Trent stopped beside Dakota, folded his arms and caught the guard's eye, putting an immediate end to the vituperative stream with a hard, unflinching glare.

The security guard looked momentarily embarrassed. "Nasty little good-for-nuttens," he muttered, as if that excused his abuse. "Bothering decent people."

The boys were standing a safe distance from the guard, and seemed to have caught on to the fact that with Trent and Dakota there, they weren't likely to get the threatened licking. They laughed and jeered. The littlest one waved at Dakota again, and this time, she waved back.

The guard huffed off, and Trent got Dakota walking again. She looked over her shoulder to catch one last look at the boys, who seemed no worse for wear. "So young," she murmured. "The little one… What's a kid like that doing out unsupervised?"

"His mom probably works, and one of the others has to watch him."

"There's nobody in the group over ten," she responded. "Who's watching *them?*"

He stopped, his face serious, his eyes searching out something in hers. She wasn't sure what that was, or whether he'd found it. "It's their way, Dakota," he said mildly.

She nodded, and didn't argue any further. As they ventured deeper into the chaos, he put one hand at her elbow, as if they were, if not friends, at least companions. She wondered why she didn't draw away from his touch.

They stopped at the main stage. This was where they would part company.

"Busy day?" he asked.

"Lots of interviews lined up. Gonna case the joint, too, chat a bit with the stagehands…" Stagehands were a goldmine of celebrity gossip. Of course, it was the kind of gossip that got people like Trent, and his clients, into deep trouble, should a writer have a mind to use it. She was definitely not comfortable discussing the details of her job with him.

"Writing up our little interview last night, too?" he probed.

She wasn't sure if he really cared or if he was just trying to needle her. "You didn't give me much to go on. Not enough for a *responsible journalistic story,* anyway." *Take that,* she thought.

He didn't seem in the least disturbed. Or, if he was, he didn't show it. "When will you be through?"

"My last meeting's at about four, so maybe around five?"

He whipped out a card as smoothly as a magician

pulling an ace from his sleeve, and handed it to her. "Call me when you're ready."

She took the card and read his name to herself as if she'd never seen it before. By the time she looked up, like a magician, he was gone.

The early evening hour didn't make the weather any cooler. Dakota picked her way through the maze of workmen erecting huge, billowing white tents over the VIP seating area. The stage was already up. The decorators were hanging a huge backdrop depicting a Tobago landscape, with an azure sea that so closely mimicked the color of the sky that the point where they met was almost seamless.

The sound system was in place, and throughout the day, Dakota had paused from her work to enjoy the megastars of the jazz world as they rehearsed. There was a huddle of people onstage, and an even larger group on the ground in front of it, filled with curious onlookers, local and foreign reporters, and workmen who couldn't resist stopping to listen.

The loudspeakers screeched, piercing Dakota's eardrums like knitting needles, until the soundman got it under control. Then a voice floated down to her, one so sweet, pure and clear that she wondered for a second if it was human. But it was, and there was no doubt who it belonged to.

Shanique.

Dakota felt the crowd around her dissipate like smoky wraiths in the light breeze. She was alone, wrapped in Shanique's perfect voice. The curvaceous diva was dressed in a shape-hugging silver jumpsuit, her thick black hair piled high in an elaborate 'do, and hoop earrings down to her shoulders, emphasizing her long neck. She was in full makeup, as if this were a dress rehearsal rather than a practice session. Dakota suspected Shanique didn't pick up the mail at the bottom of her driveway without dressing as if for a photo shoot.

Yet that voice! That blessed, God-given voice was as flawless and controlled as it had been at the height of Shanique's career. Dakota shook off a ripple of guilt. She might have been the one to expose the scandal, but she had simply written the truth. Shanique's drug abuse and the subsequent consequences were the results of her actions alone.

Dakota shifted her gaze to Shanique's entourage. She recognized Enrique Palacio, her manager; one of her personal assistants; and the festival's musical director. Then she saw Trent standing onstage, several yards away from her entourage. He was listening to Shanique, listening to her voice come through the speakers. His arms were folded, brows drawn, and he was focused on his singer as if she was the only other person there.

Slowly, his lips drew back in a smile that was clearly a mix of satisfaction, relief and pleasure. Dakota was sure she knew what he was thinking: after months of worry and anxiety, Shanique still had it. She still had the voice, the stage presence, the oomph. Dakota looked back to Trent's smiling face. His star was reborn.

His eyes flicked in her direction and locked with hers. For a second, he looked surprised to see her there, as if he'd forgotten she was at the park. She flinched, positive that her intrusion on the session would be enough to flip that smile upside down.

Instead, it grew wider. Just slightly, but those lips of his definitely twitched.

She had to resist the impulse to look behind her, romantic-comedy style, to make sure he was smiling at *her* and not someone standing at her elbow. She rewarded him with a surprised smile of her own.

He nodded a greeting—and then the singing stopped. Suddenly, jarringly, like a needle had been dragged across a vinyl record.

"What the hell is she doing here?" Shanique screamed. At Shanique's shriek and out-flung arm, all heads turned in Dakota's direction. Each pair of curious eyes was like a poisoned dart, piercing Dakota's hot, embarrassed skin. "Who said you could be here? You spying on me?"

Instinctively, Dakota's hands came up in denial, and she dropped the notebook and pens she'd been clutching. Shanique was almost six feet tall barefoot; on a stage, in heels, she grazed the sky. The woman stormed across the stage—only to catch an ankle in one of the exposed power cords. She staggered forward, and there was a collective gasp.

Shanique righted herself with exaggerated dignity, extricated her shoe from the cord, and frowned at it as if it shouldn't have been there. She kicked the cord away from herself, and in a few long stomps was at the edge, towering over Dakota. In their fury, the dark, perfect features grew even more terribly beautiful. "Did you hear me? I asked you a question!"

Trent's shadow fell across the silver jumpsuit and his hand closed over her upper arm. "Shanique," he said, softly but firmly, "calm down."

Shanique could not. "This woman's here to spy on me! She won't rest until she destroys my career!"

That, Dakota thought, was taking ego a little too far.

She recovered her composure and replied calmly, "I'm here to work, just like any other writer. I'm not here to cover you." She could have added, *unless you mess up again,* but that would have been like putting out a campfire with napalm.

Trent came to her aid. "Dakota's just doing her job, Shanique."

The coal black, silver-rimmed eyes widened. She shot Trent a look that would have paralyzed a lesser man. "Dakota? Since when are you on a first-name basis with this…*demon?*"

Declan's swear jar was how, Dakota thought, wondering if she should be more upset at Shanique's name-calling.

Trent's eyes locked with Dakota's for a moment, and then were steady on Shanique's again. "We were at the same hotel last night. We…had a conversation. She's not here for a witch hunt." His voice was soothing, mesmerizing. "Now, why don't you pick up where you left off, hmm?" He tilted his head in the direction of center stage. Shanique's entourage gave hopeful, encouraging nods. Stage time wasn't easy to come by; they had a time slot and didn't want to waste it.

Shanique wasn't letting it go that easily. "Are you kidding? I'm not singing if she's here! Why should I? So she can go back and tell her crazy readers that I'm lip-synching to some…some midget in my pocket?"

The question would have been funny, if it wasn't for the fact that there was so much hatred flowing in Dakota's direction. She was about to return fire when Trent nodded to one in Shanique's entourage. "Get her back into position, and take it from the top." Then, to Dakota, "You ready?"

Shanique's eyes became slits. "What was that?"

Trent's answer was as calm as the Dead Sea. "Dakota needs to change hotels. I offered her a lift."

Before another shriek could pierce the air, Shanique's people whisked her in one direction, and Trent marched Dakota in the other. She knew better than to resist. Together, they stepped out from under the tents and into the waning sunshine.

The park was busier than it had been that morning, with wet bars and food service areas being mounted at several points, and ticket booths at three main entryways. Trent flashed his pass at the same bull-chested security guard who had been on duty earlier. He gave them a sour look, nodded them out, then scowled in the direction of the roadway.

Dakota followed his gaze. The gang of ragged youngsters was still there, engulfed in the drama of the preparations. It was probably the most exciting thing to happen to them in…well…forever. They spotted Dakota and Trent, and their dark, sunburned faces lit up with broad grins. They poured into the street like puppies through a hole in the fence, indifferent to the heavy traffic plying the road.

"Miss! Miss! You have a dollar?" one of the taller ones asked.

"Where you from?" asked another. "Trinidad?"

"The States," she replied.

The dark eyes glinted. "American dollars, then." The children jostled, scrawny bare arms outstretched. Even the tiny one, with the deep dimple, clutched his jam jar with its long-suffering fish against his chest and held out his hand. It was obvious they were used to begging;

this was probably why the security guard was so hell-bent on keeping them away from patrons.

Compassion tore at her. They didn't look as if they were starving, not the way a child looked in a war-torn country. This was Tobago, not Somalia. However, they'd been out here all day under the merciless sun, and God alone knew what they'd had to eat or drink. When they finally made it home, she wondered, what kind of meal would be waiting for them? From the thinness of the boys' arms, her guess was not much.

She fumbled through her bag, reaching for her purse, but a hand closed over her wrist.

"Wait," Trent said.

She scowled. "I'm giving them something, Trent."

"That isn't the way—"

Typical. Spoiled city-boy executive, too rich and too self-important to remember there were people out there who didn't have steak every day. What kind of man refused to give a dollar to a hungry child? She put him firmly in his place. "It's my money. I can do as I like with it. And they're hungry!"

Behind his well-fitted designer shades, his brown eyes were calm. "I know they are. Which is why you have to trust me."

She stopped, her wallet still in one hand, unopened. The boys stood attentively around, as if wondering how the squabble was going to play out. The youngest, unable to hide his frustration, let out a whimper. Dakota's frown deepened into a glare. "Trent…"

Without answering her, he beckoned to the boys. "Come on, guys. Follow me." He threw her an amused smile. "You, too."

Puzzled, she walked beside him into a touristy

beach café painted in bright colors. The boys brought up the rear like ducklings at feeding time. Driftwood was nailed to one wall, a stuffed marlin to the other, and fishing nets festooned with shells and dried starfish hung from the ceiling like a cloudscape. A young woman, with heavy braids and a space between her front teeth wide enough to whistle through, met them halfway, her glance flicking from Trent to the boys behind him. She looked a little uncertainly at the barefoot gang bringing up the rear. Other diners turned to stare. A few soft words and a flash of Trent's credit card solved her dilemma nicely. She dragged three tables together on the patio, and the excited, laughing boys shoved and pushed for seats, each vying for the spot closest to their American benefactors.

Dakota put her purse away. Her first reaction was a sheepish *Now, why didn't I think of that?* Her second was wonder. It seemed the formidable Trent Walker liked kids. The dour Trent Walker had at least one charitable bone in his body. The frosty Trent Walker had a soft heart.

Well, if that didn't beat all.

It took three waitresses to feed them. The food kept coming, and as fast as it came, it disappeared into the bottomless pit that is the stomach of a young boy. Hot fries and battered shark fillets, red beans and rice, fatty stewed pork and thick bowls of the callaloo soup she'd sampled last night vanished almost as quickly as they were delivered. Then came dessert: ice cream like Dakota had never dreamed of: ginger-coconut, guava, avocado. All, the owner assured them, homemade in her own kitchen.

As the boys feasted to bursting, Dakota watched

Trent laugh and joke with them. They opened up, pouring out their stories. They all lived on the same street, in a village half an hour's walk away. Only one had a dad at home; the others lived with aunts, mothers and grandmothers, most of whom didn't work. The boys talked about their days swimming in the rivers or the sea, begging for tourist dollars and running errands. How most of the time, they didn't go to school because they had no shoes or books.

Trent had removed his sunglasses and was leaning forward with interest, arms folded on the table, listening. Shame rolled through Dakota. To think she had accused him, even mentally, of being a cheap, insensitive bastard! There was more to this man than she thought.

As they rose, too stuffed to eat another nibble, the owner appeared with shopping bags filled with boxed food to take to their families. By now, Dakota had gotten into the spirit of the moment, and was beaming at Trent as she handed the bags over to the surprised and delighted kids, slipping them fistfuls of candy as she did so. Trent settled the bill, and they streamed out of the café on a ripple of excited chatter.

At the side of the road, they parted company. The boys fist-bumped Trent, looking pleased with all the attention. A few of them hugged Dakota shyly. The littlest one, who she now knew was named Callum, gave her a deep-dimpled grin and held out his jam jar of fish. "*Wabine,* Miss. We catch it in the drain this morning."

"It's very pretty," she said of the lone survivor. After a day of being sloshed around and trundled about in a kid's hot hands, the poor thing looked like it just wanted someone to put it out of its misery.

"Take it," he said.

"Oh, but I—"

"Thank you, Callum," Trent interrupted, taking the fish on her behalf. "Miss Dakota will take good care of it for you."

Her eyebrows shot up, but she recovered fast. "What do I feed it?" she asked the boy.

Callum looked at her for a second, taken aback by the odd question. "Whatever you have," he said finally, with the kind of smile that was destined to melt female hearts in years to come.

Moved beyond words, Dakota stooped, threw her arms around him and kissed him on the cheek.

The cranky security guard was just going off duty; he glared at the heavy, food-filled bags the boys were holding, and then at Trent and Dakota. Trent offered an ironic salute.

"Suckers," the man mouthed, and stalked off.

The boys jabbered their goodbyes and trotted away, toting their loot. Trent and Dakota watched until they were out of sight. She was left alone with a man who, in just one hour, had turned her original opinion of him on its ear. He was easy in her presence. Relaxed… almost friendly. The journalist in her wanted to know even more.… The woman in her wasn't sure she could handle whatever knowledge she would glean.

She gave the fish a suspicious look. "How'm I supposed to take care of it?"

He stuck his nose into the bottle, pondering the creature's fate. "You can take out the dead ones, top it up with bottled water and throw it a breadcrumb every day. Or you can find a river and send him on his way."

The last suggestion was tempting. "I promised Callum."

"You did." He surrendered the jar to her and led her in the direction of his car. "You know kids. You've got to keep your promises. Bad karma, otherwise."

She'd gag on her curiosity if she didn't ask. She knew he wasn't married, but… "You have kids?"

He looked surprised by the question. "Me? No. Lots of nephews, though. Boys run in my family."

"Oh." More questions arose, but she shoved them down. Story or no story, she didn't need to know anything more about this man right now. He was dropping her off at her new hotel, and after that, she'd probably just catch a glimpse of him from the other side of the park. That was it.

She settled into the car. He consulted his map, figured out the route to the hotel, and pulled away from the curb. A comfortable silence fell, broken only by the soft slosh of water in the jar.

They turned into a dark street, lined with dying coconut trees. The car shuddered as the asphalt gave way to gravel, and the houses grew shabbier and shabbier. Dakota frowned, her internal early warning system giving a loud beep. "You sure you have the right place?"

"I think so," Trent responded. He sounded as worried as she felt. He stopped in front of the only establishment on the street that would pass for an inn. It was newer than the other houses, painted a bright green and lined with a haphazard assortment of palms, hibiscus shrubs and bushes. Cars were parked unevenly on the white gravel drive. Dub music blasted from speakers up on poles. *The Sugar Apple Inn* was hand-painted on the outer wall, in letters of varying sizes.

So it wasn't a three-star hotel. *I can do this,* Dakota thought. *Maybe the music shuts off at a reason-*

able hour. As long as the beds are clean, and the door locks, I'll be fine. "I can take it from here," she said bravely. She waited for him to open the trunk and hand her bags over.

Trent looked at her as if she was insane. "Let's take a look inside." He put his arm around her, as naturally as if he'd done it before, and guided her through the main doorway into an open courtyard. The din here was even louder. The smell of hot grease assailed them. Men stood around, local and foreign, drinking Carib beer from the bottle and grabbing handfuls of fried chickpeas from the bar.

There were just a few women present, overdressed in cheap, tight clothes and even cheaper jewelry. Some were pigeonholed by the men they were talking to, others seemed to be the aggressors, leaning against the bars, their painted lips propped into seductive smiles, the targets of their attention as mesmerized as moths in the headlights.

Bad, Dakota thought. *Very bad.*

One short, gray-faced man with unkempt hair peeled himself away from behind the bar and walked toward her. He was dressed more neatly than most of the others, and the words *Sugar Apple* were embroidered on his breast pocket, so when he was near enough, she asked, "Are you the manager?"

He frowned, like it was a hard question. "I guess." He peered at her, leaning close, looking her up and down like he was getting a deal on a secondhand car. "You the new girl?"

"Let's go," Trent said, whirling her around and heading for the door.

"Right with you," she gasped, her face hot and her

stomach cold. She walked almost faster than he did, anxious to put as much space between her and the Sugar Apple as possible. She slumped forward on the car, her forehead hitting the cool metal roof with a *thunk*.

"That wasn't a hotel." She felt his hand on her shoulder, but didn't lift her head. "That was a…"

"I know," he said sympathetically. He squeezed her shoulder comfortingly. "Don't be upset, it's…"

A bubble of emotion began rising inside her. Her shoulders began to shake. She tried again to speak, but choked on her words. Her breath came in gasps.

Trent spun her around, concern written all over his face. "It was a mix-up," he tried to persuade her. "It's no reflection on you."

And then the bubble popped, and laughter poured out. "He thought I was a…a…hooker! Can you beat that?"

The emotions on Trent's face switched from concern to puzzlement to relief. "I thought you were…"

"What?" she answered in amusement. "Crying?" She wiped a tear of mirth from her eye. "Are you kidding? That was priceless." She looked down at herself, critically assessing her smart black jeans and slightly bedraggled coral blouse. "I sure hope it wasn't something I'm wearing that…" She trailed off.

When she looked up, he was assessing her, too, but not as critically. "It's nothing you're wearing, or anything you said. The guy just…" He waved his hands helplessly. "You walked into the wrong joint, that's all."

A sobering thought was enough to still her laughter. She was back to being homeless. "Now I have nowhere to go."

The answer, the obvious answer, hung in the air

like a mist. His stare was so intense, she looked away. "That's ridiculous," she said in response to his unspoken invitation.

"Why? It's clean, safe and private."

"You'll be there," she blurted, and just barely stopped herself from clapping her hand over her mouth.

He gave a throaty chuckle. "I will, but I think I'm the lesser of the two evils."

Right on cue, the song on the loudspeaker changed to something even more lewd. The whole atmosphere made Dakota cringe. Still, she resisted. "I'd be imposing."

"You'd be more than welcome," he countered. "If you like, we can draw up a truce and sign it in blood."

She chuckled. She wasn't dumb enough to turn down this lifeline. "I… Thank you."

He hadn't put his sunglasses back on since they'd left the restaurant, so his eyes were unshielded. What she saw in them was mystifying. This was a man who didn't like her, and yet he seemed almost glad for her company.

As he held open the car door for her to sit, she was forced to ponder an even greater mystery. She didn't like him, either, so why was she so glad for his hospitality? Trying not to think too hard, she stared out of the window into the darkness as they wound their way back to Speyside…and Rapture.

Chapter 5

Trent walked alongside Dakota as they stepped into the lobby, and they were momentarily taken aback by the ruckus. Excited cheers rose above the music and laughter. Something was up. He wasn't surprised; at Rapture, something always seemed to be happening. He glanced down at Dakota, who clutched the fish jar to her bosom and climbed the stairs next to him as if she was mounting the gallows. He made her nervous.

On the surface, her wariness was mildly amusing, but it also made him sad. There'd been nothing but bad blood between them, and with good reason, he still believed. But in the short time they'd spent together he'd also discovered another side to her; one that was thoughtful, intelligent and compassionate.

He grinned to himself. The startled look in those dark eyes when he'd taken those boys to dinner had spoken volumes. Just as his opinion of her was shifting, so was *her* opinion of *him*. As he was noticing her softness and gentleness, she was discovering he wasn't the son of a bitch he knew she thought him to be. He'd be the first to admit he'd behaved badly at dinner last night. Her questions about the lip-synching scandal had stirred up his shame and embarrassment over his part in it all, which he'd been trying to bury deep in his memory. But her questions about him and Shanique, well, those had cut too close to the bone. Their romance was dead beyond resurrection, but that didn't mean he enjoyed having someone rummage through the rubble of his broken relationship looking for a good quote. Especially not someone who'd played a part in the fiasco in the first place.

But by morning he'd pulled himself together, his resentment having burned itself out overnight. He was determined to play nice; it was the only way the two of them could get through this week unscathed. Learning more about her was making it easy. Just as, he hoped, learning more about him would make her more comfortable around him. Maybe there was a chance they could meet in the middle. And if they did, then what?

Music and laughter hit them full in the face as they stepped into the dining hall, which had been bisected by an elevated catwalk. On that catwalk, a handful of female guests were standing or reclining, dressed in thong panties and little else. Each was being attended to by an artist, who was slowly and carefully painting fantasy artwork on his ticklish canvas. The women's skins had suddenly sprouted flowers, animal prints, even lizard scales.

"This place is…" Dakota fished for words. "Unbelievable," she finished eventually, but that hardly covered it. One artist, who wore nothing but cutoff jeans that revealed long, tanned legs, stopped in midstroke at their approach, and bestowed a slow smile on her. Looking startled, she smiled back.

Trent felt a growl rise inside his belly. It didn't reach his lips, but nonetheless surprised the hell out of him. He set down Dakota's bags, his body tensing.

"The ink's edible," the man said, still holding his brush aloft. The young woman he was painting pouted, her hand coming up to her hip, smudging the wild '60s tie-dye pattern. She scowled at Dakota, lip curling.

The artist gave his young lady a placatory smile. "Be right with you, honey." Then he looked Dakota up and down, brazen in his assessment. "You'd make a very good canvas, I think." He leaned closer. "I'm available for private jobs, if you desire."

Trent burned to tell this twerp that Dakota desired no such thing, then reminded himself, to his annoyance, that he didn't speak for her. Relief rocked him when she shook her head no. The artist turned back to his painting job on the inner thigh of the impatient woman, and Dakota tore her eyes away from his exposed torso, flushing in spite of herself.

There was a collective whoop as a woman, covered with painted-on butterflies, stepped down from the stage and into the arms of her appreciative lover, who planted a long kiss on her turquoise lips.

Dakota gave an audible gasp of recognition when the man squeezed past them, clutching the woman by the hand. It was the same one they'd seen last night at the table next to theirs, caressing his dining partner's nipples with his champagne glass. The man flashed a smile, eyes glowing like magnesium set alight. "Truth or Dare down on the beach tonight," he informed them gleefully. "You guys should come."

Trent gave Dakota a deliberately innocent look. "Wanna check it out?" He wondered what the stakes would be if they played *that* game together.

She shook her head, addressing the blue-eyed man rather than him. "I'm not very daring," she apologized. The amorous couple nodded sympathetically.

"A few days at Rapture will cure that," the woman said. As she spoke, her fingers trailed down the butterfly antennae painted onto her collarbone. She was in her forties, a little soft in the tummy and hips, but she wore her paint with pride, as if the atmosphere of sensuality that pervaded every particle of air they breathed had filled her with a new awareness of her body and her appetites. Her eyes glittered with the kind of satisfaction that came from being adored and sexually replete. "Just open yourself up to the magic," she added.

Trent felt his brows rise. Magic? Starlight and romance and all that?

Butterfly Lady was serious and sincere. "I mean it. These are the islands. There's magic everywhere you turn," she insisted, with no trace of irony. "Bottles and jars of weird stuff in every corner. Spirits everywhere— ask any Tobagonian. Under bushes, up in trees. You can even buy a love potion, if you know where to find one." She threw a coy glance at Trent. "Take my word for it. You won't leave Rapture the same way you came." She planted a deep kiss on her lover's lips, laughed and they ran off.

Magic, huh? Trent thought. *Sure.* He wasn't a credulous person, but didn't doubt that on an island like this people really did believe in such rubbish. He'd been around the Caribbean, Indonesia and West Africa, and knew that belief in charms and potions was alive and well. The antidote was a healthy dose of skepticism and a sprinkling of good humor.

He looked at Dakota. She was staring at the receding couple, her eyes wide. Surely she didn't…

She shifted her jar from one hand to the next and gave him a wary look. "Maybe we should…"

"Right. Back to our cabin." Ours. Strange choice of word. They'd only spent one night in the place, and he certainly couldn't consider it spending the night together, but he was already thinking of the cabin as theirs. Life sure took some strange turns. He lifted Dakota's bags once again, and together they walked through the body-painting melee and out the back door.

In the master bedroom, Dakota put her unfortunate *wabine* in its jam jar on the dresser, and topped it up with bottled water. She stripped down, feeling inadequate under the sensual stare of the wet, naked woman in the painting over the bed. What an odd day. As she undressed, her mind replayed little snippets of it; the carefree boys, Shanique spitting fire, blundering into The Sugar Apple Inn…and Trent coming to her rescue once again.

She wasn't sure what to make of the man. Why were thoughts of him taking up more and more space inside her head? Why couldn't she stop seeing his face every time she closed her eyes? In the entertainment business, his good looks were legendary. His charm even more so, although this was the first time she'd been fortunate enough to experience it first hand. But that wasn't it.

This strange attraction for Trent Walker must just

be curiosity. Nothing more. He'd cut her off from all access to him, denying her interviews and trading insults at parties. Then all of a sudden there they were, thrown together by circumstances, and in spite of herself, she was burning to know more about him…and it had nothing to do with her job.

Maybe it was the island magic.

"Yeah," she said mockingly under her breath. "That's gotta be it."

She climbed into the shower with a satisfied sigh. The powerful stream of water felt good on her tired body, soothing and invigorating at the same time. It ran into her mouth, bringing a thrill of delight. It was the sweetest tap water she'd ever tasted, almost fragrant. Or was that the perfume coming in from the garden through the antique wooden latticework along the top of the wall?

She lathered up, luxuriating in the feel of the bubbles and the silky soap as it slid over her nipples and between her thighs. She wondered briefly what design she'd pick, if she had the guts to stand on a platform in nothing but a thong and have her body painted. With edible paint, no less. What flavors did they offer? And who'd want to lick it off?

Suddenly, an image of Trent Walker in the shower with her came to mind. He was just as wet, and just as naked as she, and they watched together as the painted designs on her body softened and melted, then pooled in a rainbow stream at their feet.

Her breath caught in her throat, short and rough. The sting of the water on her nipples made them rise and harden. It coursed down the curve of her belly as she imagined his hands would. She tilted her head forward, allowing the water to soak her hair, hoping it would cool her thoughts. She turned the spray on to maximum force, shuddering under the stinging blast.

This was crazy. Fantasizing about this man like a schoolgirl. The Rapture philosophy was getting to her, with its erotic paintings and *Kama Sutra* and all this naked swimming, body painting nonsense. The entire establishment was designed for lovers and lovemaking. There was a candy jar filled with condoms in the medicine cabinet, so many that if she inflated them all she could float across the Atlantic. But that didn't mean she had to indulge in this daydreaming.

She couldn't stop fantasizing. She could feel his eyes on her, his breath. Unbidden, her hand, encased in the lathered-up bath mitt, followed the course of the water over her navel, past the bump of her belly, and slid between her legs. That first contact was a thrill.

I don't even like him, she told herself. This is stress relief, pure and simple. That's all.

But the psychic manifestation of this stunning man was pressed against her back, mouth to her ear, and her rational protests were drowned in the crash of the pounding water. The roughness of the mitt was exquisite torture against her pink, swollen flesh. She bit her lip—or did imaginary Trent bite it for her?

Stop.

Stop!

She squeezed her eyes shut, sucking in the sweet water with each ragged inhalation, hearing thunder crashing in the distance, a storm of pleasure rolling in…and then she was enveloped in utter blackness.

At first Dakota thought her imaginary lover had brought her so swiftly and conclusively to orgasm that she had blacked out. Then she put her hand up before her face, and saw nothing. The power was out. She was not losing her mind.

Thoughts churning, disoriented, she spun around, arms outstretched, trying to feel her way through the darkness, but bath goop made the floor slippery. Suddenly her feet slipped out from under her. She made a panicked grab for the shower curtain as she slammed forward face-first.

Bright, colorful bursts of pain popped at the back of her skull like paparazzi flashbulbs. Brain-numbing agony shot up her elbow, but was immediately overwhelmed by shards of pain in her jaw. She tried to extricate herself from the shower curtain that clung wetly to her, struggling like a newly formed butterfly out of a cocoon.

She didn't realize she'd let out a pained scream until she heard Trent's responding cry. He crashed through the cabin toward her. "Dakota?"

He was *not* coming in here! "Go away! I'm naked!" Her embarrassment was doubled by the memory of what she'd been doing seconds before she fell. Was there any way he could guess?

In the darkness, an even darker shadow moved. "Don't worry, I forgot to bring my night-vision goggles." His hand landed on her arm, dangerously close to her breast, and suddenly the curtain that had been her prison became her protection.

She pulled it closer. "I can get up on my own."

"You're not doing a good job of it so far. Are you hurt?"

She could feel warm liquid running down her chin, warmer than the bath water. Blood. "I'm okay," she lied. He was still reaching for her. "Don't try to pick me up! I can—"

He sighed in exasperation, and pulled back. "Have it your way. See if you can stand."

"I can stand fine." She got to her feet with difficulty, pain still leaping in her arm, eyes smarting with effort to keep from tearing up.

"Can you find your way around?"

Much as she would have loved to tell him otherwise, she had to admit, "I'm night blind." At his pause, she continued. "It's a family thing."

"I can see great in the dark—"

She yelped and pulled the shower curtain closer. "I thought you said…"

"Relax. Let me get you something to wear. You unpack your clothes yet?"

She shook her head, then vocalized her response because of the darkness. "No."

"Okay. Let me have a look in your suitcase." She heard him feel his way over to the bedroom and start rummaging through her bag. She traded her curtain for a towel, wrapped it around herself, and followed him, one hand stretched out before her. "Let's see," he was saying, "I've got a big light-colored T-shirt and… Uh, you want me to find you some panties?"

She snatched the shirt from his hands and yanked it over her head. "I don't need you to find me any damn panties." She wasn't the most systematic packer in the world; they were probably all squished into random corners of her bag. She wasn't about to go bare butt in the air to look for them. In the dark, she managed to grasp the same jeans she'd worn that day and wriggled into them, indifferent to the risk of snagging something delicate and precious as she dragged up the zipper.

"Are you decent now?"

"You tell me. You're the one who can see in the dark."

Whatever rejoinder he might have had about her decency or lack thereof would forever remain a mystery. There was a female voice calling at the door in that pretty Tobagonian accent she'd come to like so much.

"Back in a sec," he promised. She heard him thump across to the front door, and then thump back, bathed in the halo of a kerosene lamp.

Light! Thank you, Lord.

"Hotel worker," he told her, as if she hadn't guessed. "She says the power goes out all the time on the island. The hotel has a generator, but it seems to be on the blink. Someone's working to get it going."

However fast that would be wouldn't be fast enough, she thought.

Trent held the light above her head, examining her closely. The eerie glow of the lamp made him look like a sci-fi movie villain, but the concern on his face was anything but villainous. "You're bleeding all over your shirt!"

She put her hand to her chin, feeling the warm stickiness and smelling the coppery scent of her own blood. "It's nothing," she said mulishly.

"Nothing my…" He placed the lamp where it would give him the best light, grabbed her recently discarded towel and, with one hand cradling her jaw, gently tilted her head and began to dab at her wound.

"You aren't wearing gloves," she warned. "You're not supposed to mess with other people's blood."

"Got anything I can catch?"

"No."

"Then I'll just have to do the best I can." He took her hand and made her hold the towel against her chin. "Keep some pressure on it while I try to find something to stop the bleeding."

He tramped to the bathroom and threw open the medicine cabinet. "Whoa!"

"What?"

"Cookie jar full of condoms."

And there they would stay, she thought. For lack of a response, she grunted.

"These guys aren't joking about their romantic agenda," he went on, oblivious. "Did you notice the *Kama Sutra* on the nightstand?"

"Uh-huh."

He came back, first-aid kit in hand. "Ever read it?"

"Have I ever read…?"

"…the *Kama*…"

"Oh." She could feel herself blush. "Yeah, well…" She laughed a little. "Who hasn't?"

In the dark, she was sure he was smiling. "Keep your chin up," he ordered. He studied the array of bandages, then the wound under her chin, sizing it up. He began snipping away at a roll of tape.

"You seem to know what you're doing."

"When you spend as much time outdoors as I do, you'd better know a little first aid."

"You spend time outdoors?"

"Should I be insulted by your surprise?" he asked with amusement in his voice.

She began to apologize, but he held her chin firmly. She gritted her teeth as she felt the sting of alcohol, glad the discomfort distracted her from the sensation of his fingers against her skin.

"We city boys got to get out into the fresh air some-time," he went on. "I go camping whenever I can and white-water rafting two or three times a year."

"Oh," she said lamely. One more thing she'd discovered about him that she would never have imagined. She could see him, in a raft or kayak or whatever they went down rivers in, muscles straining against the raging water. And the image of surging white water took her right back to their imaginary encounter in the shower, and the reason she'd fallen in the first place. She was glad the orange glow of the lamp covered her flush.

"So, what happened?" he asked as he tapped some white powder onto a gauze pad, and pressed it against her chin. "Hold on to that while I tape it up."

"What happened? I lost my balance in the damn dark." She hoped he didn't ask how.

Luck was on her side. He satisfied himself that the bandage was neat, and then their eyes locked. "Anything else hurt?"

"Um, my arm took a whack, but..."

He immediately reached out and began feeling gingerly down it.

She tried to extricate herself. "If something was broken, I'd know."

"I guess so. Just wondering if you're still in shock."

The only shocking thing was how she was responding to his light, almost clinical touch. Like a little girl with a boo-boo that needed to be kissed. As he felt along her bruised elbow, she sucked air in softly between her teeth.

"Sore?"

Sore? Pain had not been the dominant sensation there. "Trent," she gasped.

"Yes?" he answered huskily. Something told her he understood the exact nature of the response he'd sent shooting through her. His warm palm still gingerly cupped her elbow. "Want me to get some ice for that?"

She pulled her arm away from his grasp with a mixture of reluctance and resolution. "It's...hot...in here. The air-conditioning's off," she explained hastily. "Maybe we should go out onto the patio?"

She prayed Trent couldn't guess that the heat she was experiencing had nothing to do with the tropical night.

Chapter 6

Trent tossed the bloodied towel into the laundry basket and washed his hands carefully. "I'm with you on that." He kept his tone deliberately casual, trying to mask the disturbance roiling within him. Bad enough that he'd given in to the impulse to let Dakota share his cabin, not just for the night but the entire week. But he'd be lying if he claimed that the resort's single-minded devotion to the pursuit of carnal pleasures wasn't getting to him. He half regretted choosing it. Maybe it wasn't just Dakota who was having problems finding appropriate hotels. Okay, so the name Rapture hadn't meant much when he'd given his travel agent the go-ahead to book. After all, Apple Jacks cereal didn't taste like apples.

But here he was, in a place designed for romance, with a woman who didn't like him much. Technically, he shouldn't like her, either, but minute by minute he was growing so intensely and irrationally attracted to her that he greatly doubted his ability to keep his hands off her.

It was irritating, the way she had of drawing him in. It was as if she was the moon, and he the tide, incapable of resisting her pull. He was ashamed to admit even to himself that when he'd heard her fall and had come charging in, he was more aware of the fact that she was naked than of the fact she was hurt.

And when he'd touched her, even to perform a task as mundane as bandaging a wound, he'd said a silent thank you for the darkness that hid his arousal. Now she was fixed up, and they were alone in a bedroom with a huge brass bed and a copy of the *Kama Sutra*. Removing himself from that temptation sounded like an excellent idea.

He glanced through the French doors. "It's quite light outside. The moon's not exactly full, but it's getting there. You hungry?"

She patted her stomach. "After that feast down at the beach café? Are you kidding?"

"Drinks, then. There's some pretty good stuff in the cabinet."

"Sounds great." Her response was carefully nonchalant.

She preceded him outside and he joined her quickly, armed with an Australian red wine and two glasses. He also ignored her claim of being too full to eat and brought out a small, round cheesecake that had been thoughtfully placed in the fridge, along with two forks. It was garnished with a large orange hibiscus flower. He arranged everything on a small table. Dakota perched on a hammock, bravely trying to maintain her balance, while Trent dragged a lounge chair closer.

He lit two fat, vanilla-scented candles he'd found in the kitchen and poured them each a liberal drink. She raised her glass in a symbolic toast and brought it to her lips.

Concern overrode caution. "How's your mouth?"

She paused in midsip. "What?"

"I mean… Is it sore? Injured?" He knew he sounded flustered, and that irritated him.

"Oh." She seemed to be thinking. "It's fine." Then she added with a nervous laugh, "My jaw broke my fall." Before he could say he was sorry, she took a long sip of her wine and closed her eyes. "Good," she sighed.

This was a woman who enjoyed her pleasures. He'd have to keep that in mind. They drank, listening to the rustle of the gentle wind in the leaves of the enormous tree towering above, and the cacophony of crickets and frogs. He could see by the curve of her spine as she fitted herself to the hammock that she was relaxing in his presence. Fine with him. He could get used to her company.

It was bound to happen, though, his curious nature being what it was. He took the chance of breaking up their fragile détente by announcing, "My turn."

She turned her face to him. "For what?"

"To ask questions. About you."

"You didn't complete your interview last night," she countered with spirit. "What makes you think you have the right to interview me this evening?"

He shrugged, acknowledging her point. "Not a right, but will you grant me the privilege?"

"Why?"

He shook his head slowly. "I'm not sure." Which was a lie. He knew exactly what fueled the curiosity burning within him. It was the need to better understand this complex woman, whose mere presence was making him question his usually stoic nature. He masked his uncertainty with a laugh. "You trying to tell me you can dish it out, but you can't take it?"

It was all the bait he needed. She rose to it at once. "Of course not! What do you want to know?"

She had him there. What *did* he want to know? "Anything."

"I was born—"

"And raised in Miami. You went to college in Fort Lauderdale and interned with a weekly paper there." He put his drink down and leaned closer. "You came to Santa Amata five years ago, when you were twenty-three. You've had your own column for four years. The number of papers you appear in almost doubled last year." He could have added *after the story on Shanique,* but didn't need to.

When she frowned suspiciously, he wondered if he'd gone too far.

"You researched me?"

Almost apologetically, he explained. "Only after you wrote about us. A good businessman needs to know his enemy."

The bandage under her chin wobbled. "Am I your enemy?"

"Not anymore," he realized out loud. The rational part of him knew…had always known…she'd just been doing her job. She was a respected journalist, not part of the gutter press. Even through the residue of hurt and bitterness he felt in the wake of her story, he understood that.

She drained her drink. "So if you know so much about me, why are you asking me questions?"

"Because all I have is data. Facts. I want to know about *you*."

She frowned as if thinking hard, sorting through her mental files as if trying to find a place to start. "I love music. I love writing. It made sense to put the two together and make a career out of it."

"What else do you love?" he probed. "What do you do for fun?"

She laughed. "Write more."

"Don't you have friends? Don't you go out? Date?" At this, he held his breath. Last night, she'd probed into his love life, and he'd stormed off. He couldn't rightly blame her if she did the same.

A curtain descended over her eyes as she stared off into the distance. "I haven't…seen anyone in a while."

"But you were involved."

He watched that beautiful, full pink mouth move silently as though struggling to restrain words that were trying to get out. Her thin shoulders lifted and fell under the baggy T-shirt. "Didn't that come up in your investigation?" she hedged.

"I was interested in your professional life, not your personal one." When her eyes slid away, he guessed at once that maybe the two spheres of her existence had met in the middle. "Someone in the industry," he guessed.

Her lips curved. "Our kind hardly meets anyone else, do we?"

Touché, he thought. "Recently?"

"Last year." She did not elaborate.

He exhaled heavily, trying to sort out the confusing

mix of emotions rumbling through him. He was elated to have the information: Dakota kept her personal details so close to her chest that anything he could learn about her was valuable. He felt sympathy for the hurt still alive in her eyes. Whatever had happened between her and her unnamed lover had cut deep.

But most unexpectedly and disturbingly, he felt jealousy. Jealous of someone he didn't even know, but who'd had access to her heart and her body. In what universe could that make sense? "Was it a tough breakup?"

"Is there such a thing as an easy breakup?" She busied herself with the small, round cheesecake. Like all the other dishes at Rapture, it came with a card. "Mango," she informed him. "You're going to have to help me with this. If I eat the whole thing I'd probably sink in the pool."

"I thought you weren't going in the pool."

"I'm not going in the pool *naked*."

Struggling not to let his mind wander down *that* road, he accepted the hunk of cheesecake she held out, and grasped his dessert fork. He knew the last thing she wanted was for him to persist in his line of questioning, but he couldn't stop himself.

"Where's that leave you?"

She furrowed her brow. "What do you mean?"

"How's that left you feeling about…love? Romance?"

She picked up the little card that had been tucked in with the cheesecake, and lifted the vibrant apricot-colored hibiscus in the other hand. "Tag says we're supposed to eat the hibiscus, too."

He accepted her attempt at distraction graciously, allowing her time to decide whether to answer or not. He took the flower from her fingers, enjoying the fleeting contact with her skin. He sniffed it. It smelled of noth-ing at all. He parted his lips.

"You're *not* going to put that in your mouth," she gasped.

"Life is an adventure." He took a nibble of a pa-pery petal. She watched him intently for a verdict, so he shrugged. "I've tasted more flavorful lettuce." He held it out to her.

She hesitated, and then gave a what-the-heck shrug and leaned over the table, the hammock swaying under her as she did so. She cupped his hand, and guided the large flower to her mouth. She took a bite, chewing slowly, then shook her head.

"Nothing. I wonder why they suggested it." She glanced down at their half-eaten dessert. "Maybe it enhances the cheesecake."

"Knowing this place," he said glibly, "it's probably an aphrodisiac."

"We don't need an aphrodisiac," she countered hast-ily. She drew back the hand that had been curled around his.

He let his gaze take in her alert brown eyes, the heart-shaped face framed by hair that by now had dried in the warm tropical evening. The curve of her lips and the glimmer of white teeth behind them. The small white bandage at her jaw gleamed in the half dark-ness. He sniffed the scented air: that, and her presence, were aphrodisiac enough. "No, we don't," he agreed, although he didn't mean it the way she had. The com-pulsion to kiss her was so intense he felt as though the temperature of the air around him had shot up by ten degrees.

Her flustered look told him all he needed to know:

the unconscious message he'd beamed out to her had been received. She took a swig of the wine. Her defenses were down. He was about to say something flirtatious when out of the darkness, an ungodly creature dropped down onto her. Trent watched, frozen in horror for several seconds, as a flash of green, a long scaly tail, and arching claws obscured her terrified face.

She was galvanized into action, writhing and yelling as she lurched off the porch and bolted down the path with Satan's serpent clinging to her head. Trent regained his senses and ran after her, down the steps and out into the night.

By the time he caught up, she was screaming blood-chilling shrieks of pure terror. The moon was partly obscured by clouds and stars, painting the sky shades of blue, silver and gold. Enough light filtered down to let him see the beast clearly. It was an iguana, a hellishly big one, and it was terrified of Dakota. It clung to her face and hair, claws grasping, spines erect, while she spun in mad circles, pulling ineffectually at it.

"Stop," he instructed. "Hold still."

"Are you crazy? Get it off me!"

"I'm trying." He wrapped his arms around her, trying to pin her down. They were under the huge samaan tree; its red flowers dripped like blood. Rough roots protruded from the ground, some more than a foot high, threatening to send them crashing; man, woman, iguana, all. "Steady," he urged softly. "Easy."

She was panting like a racehorse, eyes bulging in horror. In spite of her petrified twisting and darting, he was able to encircle the beast's thick waist. It bucked under his hands, sending Dakota into another orgy of shrieks. "Let me…" he puffed, "I'm trying not to hurt it—"

"You're trying not to hurt *it?*"

He had to stifle a nervous laugh at her indignation. "I just want to make sure you both get out of this unscathed," he told her. The animal swiveled its eyes in its sockets, watching him warily without turning its head. Then the brilliant green monster allowed him to pry it free from its precarious position on the top of Dakota's head, reluctantly relinquishing her curls.

He avoided the razor-sharp teeth as it whipped and thrashed in his hands. Although the animal was a vegetarian, it would do what any creature would when cornered, and he wasn't in the mood to nurse a bite from a frantic reptile. He moved some distance away and released it. Once on solid ground, it bobbed its head, almost in acknowledgment, and then darted off into a patch of magenta ginger lilies, long tail rustling in the dried leaves.

He returned to Dakota to find her rooted, visibly shaking. Without hesitating, he put his arms around her. Her entire body vibrated against his. "Easy," he soothed again. "Calm, now."

Calm was the last thing she wanted to be. "A damn crocodile just fell out of the sky, and you expect me to—"

"Iguana," he corrected instinctively.

"It could have bitten my head off."

He considered explaining that the creature, as scary as it had been, was nowhere near big enough to perpetrate any such damage, but decided it was the wrong time and place for a zoology lesson.

It was, however, definitely the time and place to hold

her. Her panting had slowed; those high, round breasts of hers no longer heaved against his chest. But she seemed glad for his touch, and he was glad to touch her.

Just then, in a bid for the Good Timing of the Year Award, the lights at the resort flickered and came on. *Well, that's it,* he thought. *Game over.* "Either the power's back, or they were actually able to get that damn generator running," he commented, trying to mask his irritation at the fact that his role as comforter was becoming unnecessary, and any second now, he'd have to let her go.

She made no effort to move away. Instead, she shivered. He could smell the shampoo in her hair as it brushed against his face in the light breeze. Lilies, or something. "Cold?"

She tried to laugh. "In the Caribbean? Are you kidding?"

"You're shivering. You're in shock," he murmured. "Maybe you should lie down." He tried not to think about the fact that she wasn't wearing panties under her jeans.

That thought was interrupted by the tinkle of wind chimes. They looked up. An array of bamboo, pottery and glass chimes swayed above them. The tree's branches extended outward, a welcoming gesture, like those of a woman begging her lover to fall into her arms.

"Magic," he murmured.

"Huh?"

"Those bottles and chimes. Charms. You see them in different parts of the world. Some for the evil eye, some for good luck."

"Love charms?"

He laughed softly. "Considering where we are, I'm betting on it."

She lifted her eyes to the jangling chimes, wary but curious. He wondered if she believed in them. He knew that luck was what you made it. And so was love. *Dammit,* he thought. It was now or never. Her face, still tilted toward the chimes, was open to him. He knew exactly what she would taste like seconds before his lips landed on hers. Red wine and mangoes. A warm sweetness all her own.

Immediately, her lips parted and softened, opening for him. When the tips of their tongues touched, he felt as if someone had tossed a transistor radio into his bathtub. The jolt was so sharp it almost singed his hair. He felt her sigh softly into his mouth.

He let one hand rise to cup her pointed chin, but was reminded of her injury by the roughness of the bandage.

"Sorry," he murmured, taking his hand away.

She grasped it and rested it lightly against her cheek, nestling into it. Wisps of hair brushed the backs of his fingers. She broke their kiss only long enough to suck in a single breath, and then her sharp front teeth raked his lower lip.

He backed her up to the rough tree trunk, glad that its solidity allowed her to bear his weight as he leaned against her. He was rock hard, and because of his height, his erection pressed against the softness of her stomach. He wanted her to feel the silent message he was sending.

She heard him loud and clear. She mewed and pressed back, rising on tiptoes to try to make more intimate contact with the insistent bump, while arching her neck so as not to break the kiss.

Impatiently, he lifted her up, setting her down atop

one of the samaan's high, protruding roots; nature's own footstool. Now they were level. He grasped both cheeks of that firm, full butt he'd been admiring so much and pulled her against him. He was dead on target, pressed against her pubic bone and the crazy heat rising from it.

"My God," she gasped.

He felt one hand behind his head, making sure he didn't let up. The other was at the small of his back, snaking into the waistband of his jeans. She yanked up the tail of his shirt, exposing a strip of skin, and raked her fingernails across it. He almost lost it right there.

His name was an exhalation hissing from between her lips. "Trent."

Stupid T-shirt. No buttons down the front. He had to roll it up to gain access to her breasts. She hadn't been able to locate a bra in the dark, so they were bare to him. Her nipples were as hard as gemstones, rough against his palms. She bucked as he bent to kiss one of them.

"Trent—Trent—Trent…" She almost lost her footing on the tree root.

He held her steady, lifting his head to look into eyes that were aflame with hunger. "Stop?" he asked.

"No. Yes. I…no."

He smiled, understanding her dilemma. "Keep on?" he asked gently. He chided his body, commanding it to be patient while she cleared her thoughts. *Let it be yes,* he prayed, although he knew he'd defer without complaint if her answer wasn't what he wanted to hear.

"I didn't expect this," she puffed. Her mouth was swollen and red. Her dimples looked deep enough to sink a fingertip into.

"I know, but it's good, isn't it?"

Her hips pressed against his, heat radiating from her

core against his hardness. "Yes." She sounded as though the admission took a toll on her pride. Her hand was still down the back of his jeans. She scratched a nail along the top of his glutes again. He shut his eyes.

When he opened them, she was gazing behind him, to the pool of light on the tiny patio.

"Want to go inside?" he asked.

She looked like it took her a lot to answer. "I think… we…yes."

Hiding his disappointment, he took hold of her hand as they picked their way over the roots. The wind chimes serenaded their departure. They left the glasses and remnants of the cheesecake where they were, stepped inside and shut the door. Trent rammed the bolt home. Dakota was near enough for her body to brush his as he turned to her. She still hadn't relinquished his hand. Her face was inscrutable.

The door to the master bedroom was slightly ajar, the bed still strewn with clothes in her haste to get dressed during the blackout.

He ached with thwarted desire, but respected her decision. He verbalized her unspoken excuse. "Kinda fast, huh."

"Uh-huh," she murmured.

"It would be insane."

This time, she only nodded.

Reluctantly, he bent down, placing the lightest, gentlest of kisses on the tip of her nose. Then he straightened up. If he had to have the strength to walk away from this absurdly desirable woman, he was going to have to do it fast. "Sweet dreams," he whispered. He spun around with almost military precision, and headed for his room.

The husky velvet of her voice stopped him in his tracks. "Trent Walker," she whispered, "where the hell do you think you're going?"

Chapter 7

The look of puzzled surprise on Trent's face reflected Dakota's own feelings. She put her hand on the doorknob to steady herself. Her heart pumped insanely, and her thoughts whirred.

He stood stock-still in the corridor, unsure. "I thought you meant for us to go to our rooms. Our *separate* rooms."

Was that what she'd meant? Her fuzzy thoughts wouldn't stay still long enough for her to be certain. "Maybe I did. I don't know. But I…if you want to…you can come in." She tilted her head in the direction of the bedroom behind her. "For a…while," she added lamely.

His face was serious. He walked slowly back toward her, along what seemed like a hundred yards of corridor. "You have to be sure."

When he stood before her, the only thing between him and the huge bed in the room was her. She inhaled and held her breath, then let it ooze past her lips as she asserted, "I'm sure."

He didn't move. She was flooded with uncertainty and mortification. Had she misunderstood? Why wasn't he touching her like he had outside?

"Do you really want this?" he asked.

Want this? He was the only thing she could think of since the moment he'd stepped onto that plane. He'd irritated her, intrigued her, impressed her, but most of all, he'd fascinated her. Everything from the way he walked to the way he talked, the way he smiled and the way he touched her, only made her want him more. All evening she thought of nothing but the fact that she wasn't wearing any bra or panties, and just how easy that would make it if she chose to say yes.

There were a dozen reasons why he wasn't right for her, and a few more why sleeping with him would make her job harder. But she wanted him, anyway. Maybe it was the island air. The damn hibiscus petals they'd munched on. The painting on the wall, the *Kama Sutra* on the table, the long sexual famine she'd endured since her last relationship. But oh, yeah, she wanted him.

"I do," she choked out.

"Do…?" A ghost of a smile hovered around his lips.

"Want…this." *Want you.*

Now the smile was full-fledged. He slid his arm around her waist and eased her backward a few steps so he could shut the bedroom door. Even though there was no one else in the cabin, he locked it. The soft click was like the crash of metal in her head.

The curve of his mouth made that delicious mole on his lower lip even more prominent. It was like a punctuation mark that brought certainty to his smile. Then she couldn't see it anymore because he was kissing her. The sharp stabs of pleasure that had run through her under the big sprawling tree were back again, shredding away at her resistance like knives.

They moved toward the bed as they kissed, taking slow, steady steps. He led her as though they were dancing. Then she felt the solidity of the mattress against the backs of her thighs, and she could go no farther.

"Shirt's way too big for you," he muttered as he pulled it up over her head. "Probably way too big for *me.*"

"I sleep in it," she reasoned.

"You're not sleeping in anything tonight." He tossed the shirt onto the floor.

If she hadn't been in the Caribbean, she would have blamed the excruciating tautness of her nipples on the cold. The hard, dark nubs pointed at him, knots of excitement. He took in the sight of them, stroking her repeatedly from shoulder to nipple, and then, fanning out his fingers, lightly cupped both breasts. The palms of his hands were rough against her skin, and she wondered briefly how a pampered city boy like him got hands as rough as those. Then she remembered what he'd said about camping, rafting and all that macho jazz. Well, whatever those hands had done for him in the wild was nothing compared to what they were doing to her now.

She longed to touch him as he was touching her. She ached to see his bare back. What would his nipples be like? As tiny as dimes or as fat as quarters? Were they sensitive? If she flicked her tongue against them, or drew them between her teeth, would he cry out?

His mouth was close to her ear. "You can touch me, you know. It's allowed."

"Funny."

"I'm not joking."

He could have taken his own shirt off, but she sensed he wanted her to do it for him. It was flecked with droplets of her blood from her injury. She touched one with a curious finger. It was already dry. When she worked the polo over his head, he didn't resist.

Oh, man; he had a body on him. Not a four-days-a-week-at-the-gym kind of body, but the kind a man got overcoming the challenges of the outdoors. His glowing skin was speckled with dark hairs that swirled around large, coppery nipples, down across abs that were the dictionary definition of washboard, and then swooped into the waistband of his jeans.

Experimentally, she reached out with her left hand and grazed a thumbnail across the taut circle of his nipple.

"Yeow!"

Sensitive, she noted with a grin. Good.

They were chest to chest, rough hair against soft skin. Hands roaming, seeking, discovering. Then he pulled away. "One sec," he grunted. And he was gone.

What the...?

Then he was back again, and what he held in his hands made her laugh out loud: the entire jar of Rapture condoms. "You got high hopes."

"I'm an ambitious guy," he shot back. He set the jar down on the table.

The moment of levity chased away the last vestiges of worry and doubt, like a brisk wind sending gray clouds fleeing. "Jeans," he said.

"What about them?"

"They're in the way."

"Take yours off, then."

"Take yours off first."

"I've got nothing on under."

He grinned. "That's the point."

Not fair. She'd be stark naked; he'd still have on his boxers. Disadvantage to the home team. "Everything off, on three?"

"Deal." He began unbuckling his belt. She wasn't wearing one. "Count it," he suggested. He popped the button on his fly.

She did the same. "One…" She was so excited her toes tingled. "Two…" Now the fire was coursing up her legs. "Three!" And the last of their clothing hit the floor.

She wouldn't have been able to tear her eyes away from the spot she was staring at if there was a gun to her head. He was as aroused as it was possible to get, his long, thick shaft jutting out from a crisp bush of dark pubic hair, pointing right at her, signaling its intent. As thick as her wrist, clean, inviting, mouthwatering.

Jackpot.

He moved first, lifting her up and giving her a long, deep kiss before plopping her onto the high bed and clambering on after her. Then he took up the jar of multi-colored condoms and dumped them unceremoniously onto her tummy. "Lady's choice."

She sat up, giggling. "That's like taking me to a candy store and asking me to pick just one flavor of jellybean." She riffled through their treasure trove with her fingers. "Ribbed. Strawberry. Extra-large." She shot a brazen look at his crotch and put the last-mentioned packet on her pillow. "Better hang on to that one."

He chuckled.

They made their selection, and she helped him get it on, enjoying the chance to touch him there so intimately for the first time. "What do we do with the rest of them?" she asked, indicating the tumultuous array of packets scattered across the big bed.

He laid her on her back, hovered over her, and then settled himself down. "Pretend they're rose petals."

Rose petals. What a dreamy idea. Quirky, romantic... But this wasn't romance; this was sex. This was two adults who'd been circling around each other giving in to the undeniable urge that had possessed them from the get-go. She knew with every fiber in her being that tonight's coupling with Trent would bring her great pleasure, but when it was over, that was all it would be. This pleasure would simply satisfy a physical need.

But then he was kissing her again. Light, achingly sweet kisses on her cheeks, across her jaw, from lips to forehead. His fingers fluttered along her throat like butterflies. "Tell me," he whispered, "what's your pleasure?"

A hundred images flooded her brain at the same time, of all the things she wanted to do with him. Sensory overload. She was so consumed by the erotic possibilities open to her that she couldn't unstick her tongue from the roof of her mouth.

So he answered for her, letting his fingers skitter down her belly, and farther down until they disappeared into her wetness. She bucked against him at first contact. "This?"

Lazily, as if he had all the time in the world, he sucked a nipple in between his teeth and ran his tongue across its tip. "This?"

"Trent," she grunted. "If you don't stop, you're gonna send me over the edge right now."

"S'okay. I'll just have to haul you up and send you back over again. And again." A second finger joined the first inside her, and a shriek tore from her throat. She clapped a hand over her mouth to keep the sound in, shocked at herself.

"Relax," he whispered. "Nobody can hear you." Without waiting for a response, he curled his fingers inside her, twisting his wrist to get her just at the right angle, and began pumping his hand in and out in an ever-increasing tempo until she was writhing under him, half in an effort to get away and half in an attempt to get closer.

Sweat broke out on her skin like a fevered rash. Seismic jolts of pleasure pounded up through her core. She clawed at the sheets, feeling the plastic and foil wrappings of their pretend rose petals crinkle under her fingers. "Oh, oh, oh…"

Before the jolts could subside, he'd scooted up so he was sitting next to her, reaching for her and lifting her up. "Trent, wait…"

He was positioning her over him, on her knees facing him, one big hand steadying her hips, the other grasping his thick shaft and preparing to enter her. The idea of his penetrating her like that was enough to send another orgasm thundering through her. If he didn't let her get a grip on herself, she was sure to die.

"Trent, for the love of…"

"Hmm?" It was all he could manage with a mouth full of her breast.

"…let me catch my breath."

His sharp front teeth were torment.

"Just ten seconds. Let me get back to normal."

"No deal," he said, and thrust deep into her.

Even with the air-conditioning on full tilt, she was drenched in sweat. Intense sexual excitement robbed her of speech; she was only able to express her pleasure in guttural cries and low-pitched moans. Fortunately, it was a language he spoke fluently.

That night, she learned that hiking or camping or kayaking and whatever the hell else he did gave a man endurance. It taught him the single-mindedness required to focus on nothing else but achieving his objective. And, praise the angels, his sole objective was her pleasure.

When they finally gave in to exhaustion, in the early hours of that silvery Caribbean morning, she felt his sweat-slicked body settle against hers, and his heavy head fall upon her shoulder. She yearned for sleep. Her eyelids were weighty, her thoughts already rambling along pleasure-tinted dream paths, but she was afraid to close her eyes. What if these few moments were the only intimate ones she'd have with him? Wouldn't it be stupid to waste them? What if she fell asleep and he took advantage of that fact to slip away?

Stay, she willed him, *stay.* But she was too much of a coward to voice the words.

The rise and fall of his breath against her chest was so soothing, so comforting, that she wished she could drift off to its rhythm, confident that she would wake to feel his heart still pounding against her chest. But any second now, she knew, she would feel the shifting of his weight and the dip in the big bed as he roused himself to leave her. To go back to his room where he belonged. She felt lonely already.

That parting never came. Instead, to her astonishment, the steady hum of the air-conditioning was joined by the low rumble of his snores.

Trent Walker had fallen asleep in her bed.

Surprised, yet pleased for some reason, Dakota gingerly turned her body until she was comfortable, not daring to break contact with his. As she rested her head on his shoulder, he grunted, his heavy arm falling around her waist, and then she was cocooned in a warm embrace. Her first instinct was to fight sleep, to give herself time to savor the novelty of his embrace, as well as the strange irony of having slept with the enemy—and allowing him to rock her world.

Her eyelids fluttered shut, and, nestled in Trent's arms, she welcomed sleep.

Chapter 8

Dakota awoke to a loud cawing overhead, and a thumping and bumping that rolled from one end of the roof to the other. It sounded as though small creatures were reenacting the gang rumble from *West Side Story*. She frowned, puzzled.

"Parrots," came a voice in her ear. "Fighting for food."

If her skin wasn't firmly attached, she'd have jumped out of it. He was still there! Why hadn't he pulled the post-coital disappearing act that men were so good at?

Then a draft of cool air, wafting across her bare breasts, shoved that thought into second place. She was as naked as the day she'd graced the planet with her presence. What was more, he was naked, too.

She snatched up the cotton top sheet and hastily covered herself, flushing like a maiden with exposed petticoats. He noted the gesture, and his lips curved in a bemused, questioning smile.

"Didn't mean to embarrass you."

"You didn't," she lied, and pressed the sheet around herself even tighter.

Instead of pointing out how loudly her actions contradicted her words, he got up, located his shorts from amidst the rubble, and pulled them on. Then he followed with his polo shirt. Only when he was decently clad did he come to sit next to her again.

She eyed him warily, like the very last lobster in the tank at the Shellfish Shack.

He tilted his head slightly to one side. "You okay with this?"

"Why wouldn't I be?"

"Just asking." His voice was steady, lacking any note of defensiveness. "It was never my intention to make you feel…awkward." While he let her ruminate on that, he busied himself gathering up the assortment of still-sealed condoms-slash-rose petals that were liberally strewn about the bed, clinging to her skin, and tangled in her dark hair.

"Seemed like a good idea at the time," he murmured with a hint of humor.

"What did?"

"Well, I was specifically referring to the harebrained impulse to toss these around." He set a double fistful of bright packets down on the nightstand. "But I guess I could expand that comment to include…everything that happened last night."

"Huh," she answered noncommittally.

"Do you still think it was a good idea?"

"The condoms?"

He brought his lips close to her ear. "The sex."

"Do you?" she hedged.

"Fervently. Quit stalling."

"I…enjoyed it," she hesitated.

"Me, too, but that's not the same thing." He reached out and caressed her jaw, gently retaping a corner of her bandage. "I don't want any shadow hanging over what we did."

Shadow? Was he kidding? There was a storm front brewing. The man was like a sexual lightning rod. She felt it every time she looked at him. Every woman felt it. She remembered the happy bunny-girl on the plane, the one he'd given a backstage pass to. *He's off da hook,* she'd told Dakota with a gleam in her eye, before announcing her intention to bonk Trent silly the moment she got the chance.

Head bent, she threw him a covert look, reexamining the long, slightly craggy lines of his face, the crisp cut of his hair, and the small mole at the corner of his mouth that she'd flicked her tongue against so sensuously. This man would never find himself short of willing females. Even though he'd stuck around and slept in her bed, that wasn't to say their lovemaking had meant anything to him. The idea that she might rank among his parade of eager groupies made her gut tighten. Even worse, what if he thought she'd slept with him because she had feelings for him?

Pride made her stoic. She sat up straight—clinging to the bedsheet shield she'd put between them—and asserted coolly, "Trent, believe me, I'm fine. I'm not in the habit of sleeping around, but, well," she gave a laugh that she hoped sounded just casual enough, "I have had one or two of these in my lifetime."

"One or two of what?"

"One-night stands."

Something flickered across his face, an emotion or a reaction, but it was gone too quickly for her to identify. "That's what this was?"

Wasn't it? What had he thought...? "Uh, I..."

He had gathered the last of his clothing into his arms. His expression was neutral. "We've way overslept. If we plan on getting anything done today, we'd better get going."

The abruptness with which he got up belied his expression, letting her know without words that her struggle to keep things casual had come across as careless and brutal. *Oh, God,* she thought, *I've hurt his feelings.*

As he unlocked the bedroom door, he turned slightly to fire off his parting shot. "Could have been worse, I guess." Without waiting for her to ask, he clarified. "It could just have been research for another story.... On me, this time."

She gasped in horror. "Trent, I would never...!"

But he was out the door, his bare shoulders square. She stifled the urge to run to him, stuttering apologies and protests of innocence. The last thing on her mind last night was a story. How could he even think that? And how could she have guessed that he'd invested some sort of...emotion...into their encounter? They barely knew each other. They didn't even *like* each other all that much. Did they?

She heard the firm click of his bedroom door and then, moments later, a soft hum as the water heater kicked in, signaling that he'd stepped into the shower. She'd lost her chance. She let the sheet fall to her waist

and propped her elbows onto her knees. Her head fell
into her hands.

Nice job, Merrick.

Twenty-five minutes later, after sprinkling a few
crumbs into the water for her *wabine,* Dakota joined
Trent at the door. They followed the winding path back
to the main building from their cabin, walking shoulder
to shoulder in uneasy silence. The paradox was enough
to drive her crazy: hours ago, they were wrapped around
each other, limbs entwined, mouth against mouth, and
now the few inches between them was a no-man's-land.
She longed to say she was sorry for her insensitive comment, and assure him that she would never use their intimate encounter as fodder for her column, but held back,
in part because she was sure that raising either subject
again would be like wriggling in quicksand; the more
she struggled, the deeper she would sink. Secondly, she
could find no words to discuss their unexpected—but,
to be honest, much enjoyed—night of sex. What did
you say the morning after you slept with a man who
was supposed to be your foe?

He was polite, but reserved, pointing out the birds
pecking at the exotic fruit weighing down the branches.
At one point, a large ground lizard, well over a foot
long, darted from under a bush and scrabbled across
her sandaled feet, almost setting off a flashback of the
night before.

"Easy," he murmured comfortingly. His gentleness
was surprising, considering how mad he must be at her.
"He's a whole lot smaller than your iguana."

"He's still a whole lot bigger than any lizard I've
ever seen," she grumbled. "Not too sure how much of

this…wildlife…I can stand." She'd been here all of two days, but already she was convinced there were a few drawbacks to island life. Back in the States, the likelihood of a humongous lizard trying to eat your head was pretty slim.

At the top of the steps, a smiling woman called out to them. "Trent and Dakota, I'm guessing?"

Trent smiled easily and held out his hand. "That's right."

"I'm Anke, Declan's business partner."

Dakota hoped her double take wasn't too obvious. She knew Declan had a partner, but of all the women who roamed the premises, she wouldn't have pegged the one standing before her as the owner of a sex-saturated island getaway like Rapture.

Anke looked about fifty. She'd coaxed her wispy ash-blond hair into thin dreadlocks that hung to her waist, with the exception of the overlong bangs falling into her glacier-blue eyes. Her skin had the kind of deep-down tan that spoke of years in the Caribbean, but she had a Nordic quality about her that made it obvious she wasn't of the island. Dakota warmed to her at once.

She took Trent's hand and squeezed it, her broad grin revealing a disarming space between her front teeth. Her accent was a medley of island music and a heavy Scandinavian baseline. "So glad to have you with us. I'm sorry I wasn't able to meet you yesterday. Did you two spend a good night?"

"Sublime," Trent responded demurely.

If Dakota's face got any hotter, a person could light a cigarette by touching it to her cheek. She gave a small nod.

"Wonderful. If there is anything at all we can do to

make your stay even more pleasurable," she paused to grin at Dakota in an I-got-your-back-sister sort of way, "please let me know."

Trent had the temerity to ask Dakota, "Was there anything you wanted last night that you didn't get?"

She could have left it at that, let him have his little laugh at her expense, but she wasn't the type to take a shot without returning fire. "Oh," she responded airily, "there's lots of time to get acquainted with all the island has to offer. I'm sure there are experiences to soak up and—" she couldn't keep her smile down "—native dishes to sample."

He was unperturbed. "Make sure you don't tangle with anything that doesn't agree with you," he warned.

"I think I can handle it," she informed him smartly.

"Good," Anke responded, oblivious to the undercurrents. "I'll be looking after you this morning. Declan's out taking Malcolm for a walk."

"You have a dog?" Dakota asked. She could imagine how happy a friendly hotel dog would be here, with an entire estate to roam and crabs to chase on the beach.

"An iguana," Anke informed her blithely. "A really big one."

"We've met him," Trent said.

"Isn't he magnificent?" Anke's purple cotton peasant skirt swirled around her ample hips as she swung around. "Now, come. We serve breakfast until quite late. Some of our guests don't emerge until almost noon." She laughed, and a starburst of creases radiated from the corners of her mouth and eyes. "You can take as long as you like over your meal, and have unlimited helpings of whatever you wish. If you have a special order, our cooks would be happy to—"

Trent cut her off with a smile. "Thank you, Anke, but I think we'll just have a quick plate and be on our way."

"Jazz, huh?"

"Yep. Dress rehearsal today."

"I think the concert's going to be great. I hope I can run away and catch a show." She gestured toward the long buffet table on one side of the room. "Enjoy," she said, and then added, "if you're interested, we have Tantric yoga classes at four and six this evening. I also do sensual couples' massages.… You can call my extension." She twinkled at them. "I promise you: if you're not in love when you get here, you will be when you leave." With that, she swirled away in a cloud of fabric.

"Huh," Dakota couldn't stop herself from saying aloud. Why did everybody assume they were a couple? Sure, it was a couples' resort, but still… Then it struck her that, despite all the space she and Trent were carefully maintaining between them, you'd have to be blind not to notice the sexual tension that arced only between people who have been sexually intimate. She might as well have a neon sign flashing above her forehead saying, "This man had me every which way last night—and I loved it." She *huhed* again.

"What?"

She shook her head and buttoned her lip. "Nothing." She let him follow her to the buffet.

As Trent drove toward the festival venue, he listened once again to Dakota as she filled the void with her chatter. Yesterday, she'd been just plain uneasy in his presence because of their hostile history, and because of how he'd stormed off from the dinner table the night before. That, he hoped, was now water under the bridge.

Today, listening to her yakking about the fish vendors and the smell of the sand, he felt as if every word was a picket hammered into the fence she was building between them. It was as if she was using her normal, everyday voice to erase from both their memories the sound of her other voice, the one only a lover was allowed to hear. The low, guttural moan she'd used to urge him to go faster, slam into her harder. The rasp in which she'd called out to all the gods in heaven, and pleaded for him to put her out of her misery with hard, well-timed thrusts.

What an amazing experience to be inside her. Sweat beaded at his temples. He'd had a niggling awareness of his attraction for her all along, and like any man in the presence of a beautiful woman, had entertained a few idle fantasies about peeling away her layers of cool to get at her heated center. But he hadn't truly expected her to reciprocate, especially not so ardently.

He'd been shocked at her response, her willingness—no, her eagerness—to let him touch her, taste her, everywhere. So soft and warm and feminine. It made him wonder why he'd thought of her as such a cold fish, a flint-hearted story hound who thought of nothing but herself and her career.

He'd barely held on to his composure when she made the comment about one-night stands. He'd been so into her that the sexual pleasure had left him with a euphoric, emotional high. Dakota was beautiful, smart and complex, and now that he was getting to know her, he couldn't get her out of his head. He liked what he knew and wanted to know more.

Finding out that it hadn't been the same for her had been a bite in the butt. That dreamy, hungry look in her eyes, the way her dark ones had held his, and the desire he'd seen in them during their heated coupling, had been inspired by a purely physical need. She might have enjoyed his body, as he had enjoyed hers, but she wasn't sweet on him. She'd obviously allowed him to scratch an itch in a spot she couldn't reach, and that was all there was to it.

The hurt had been enough to make him lash out with the accusation that she was mining their night together for a scandalous story. That was totally unfounded... wasn't it? Dakota would never do that...would she? Certainly not, he told himself firmly, because that was what he wanted to believe. It was just as she'd said. Sex for pleasure, and nothing else.

He glanced at her quickly. What had he expected? She was, after all, in the entertainment business. Sex was part of the industry's currency, along with drugs, alcohol and having a good time. He was honest enough to admit that when he'd first arrived on the scene, he'd availed himself of the bountiful offers that the groupies, party girls and songstresses threw at him, but experience and wisdom had made him more careful. He wasn't a man for playing games.

But Dakota? He had no idea. Just because he'd indulged in her body didn't mean he knew who she was. Maybe flings were her thing. Or maybe it was just the influence of the resort, with its *Kama Sutras* and nude paintings and Tantric every damn thing. Had he and Dakota fallen under some kind of Rapture spell? And, if so, would it last long enough for him to ease himself into her lush, hot body again before they left?

If it didn't, he would cast a spell of his own. Trent wasn't a man who gave in to the fickle Fates. He'd mastered the art of getting what he wanted, both in business and in life, and if he didn't have Dakota Merrick gasping out his name in orgasm at least one more time before he got on that flight, he was personally sending his man-card back to headquarters. One-night stand? Oh, no, sister.

The conversational tsunami came to an end. Dakota panted a little, trying to catch her breath. "You're not saying much," she commented.

Didn't let me get a word in, he could have told her, but instead he said, "Sorry. My mind sort of drifted."

"Where to?" she dared ask, but he had a feeling she already knew. The look she threw at him from behind her sunglasses spoke volumes, as did the fingers that self-consciously trailed along the tops of her breasts as if she was recalling the kisses he'd planted there. The knowledge that she was thinking of him was enough to make him instantly hard.

The sight of her, stroking the tops of her breasts as he had last night, drew his attention, and he took his eyes off the road for a moment—a bad thing to do along a winding, rocky coast. He swerved slightly off the narrow road and, with a screech of brakes, stopped on the shoulder.

Dakota was thrown against the passenger-side door, but she quickly righted herself. "You okay?" Dakota asked, frowning up at him.

He was overcome by embarrassment. "Uh, I'm fine. I just…" Dammit. If that happened again, they'd both wind up in an accident. Keeping his aching need for her bottled up was as dangerous as driving under the influence. He might as well let it out. "I was thinking about you. You and me, actually."

The tops of her breasts took on a rosy flush under her fingers, but she played hardball anyway. "What about me and you?"

He popped the buckle on his seat belt and slid sideways, so the steering wheel was no longer an impediment. "This."

Her mouth under his was a soft, sweet reminder of what she had felt like wrapped around him last night. Her tongue had been so skilled, and so intuitive, it seemed to have a sentience all its own. He remembered how her sucking lips and hard little teeth had reduced him almost to tears.

Now her mouth opened up under his probing, allowing him entry. *His* tongue knew a few maneuvers of its own, too. He drew her lower lip in between his teeth, his hand sliding up to cup the base of her skull to keep her where he wanted her.

A sigh escaped her. She tried to press against his chest, but the seat belt held her back. Irritated, he yanked on it, so intent on freeing her so he could crush her to him that he completely forgot the mechanics of the clasp. With a low laugh, she released it, clambered over the emergency brake, and renewed their contact.

He slid his hand up and ran his thumb against the rough diamond of her nipple. It was like flicking on a switch that led directly to the tight space between her thighs. Her body bucked like she'd been shot, and she let out a sharp, shocked cry.

He didn't want to break the kiss to speak, so he said what he had to directly against her lips. "I'm putting you on notice."

"Wh-what?"

Her breasts were full, round and firm, like the sweet,

pink grapefruit they'd had for breakfast. "S-s-something I have to tell you." Desire made him stutter as badly as she.

She opened her eyes with effort. Her pupils were wide enough to swim in. "Tell me."

His answer was a dangerous growl. "I don't do one-night stands."

Her soft laugh was pure liquid. "I'm sorry. I—"

"No apologies. Just take warning, and be ready for me."

Something in the curve of her lips told him she was ready for him now. If he didn't have a schedule to stick to, he'd have turned the car around and sped back to Speyside, where they'd spend the day cocooned in Rapture, with its vine-kissed privacy and single-minded agenda of sexual escapism.

Loath to pull away, he pressed his lips against hers again—but was interrupted by a low chuckle at the window. Startled, Trent looked up to see an angular old woman in a faded cotton dress, with her face plastered to the glass.

Dakota rocketed back into her seat and folded her arms to cover the hard points of her nipples poking through her shirt. Her eyes were bright with shock.

Unperturbed, the woman grinned, showing a row of knobby teeth. She tapped on the window with a thin hand, fingers clubbed by arthritis. When neither of them responded, she knocked again, and held up the other hand, which clutched a fistful of bright beaded jewelry.

Sighing, he slid the window down. Dakota gave him a startled look, as if she'd never expected him to acknowledge the intrusion.

"Mr. Gentleman, buy something nice for the lady?"

Her voice had a surprisingly youthful quality to it, warmed by the island sun.

He shook his head firmly, not wanting to look at the clacking bunch of touristy nonsense. "Thank you, no."

Undaunted, she persisted. "Miss Lady, let your husband get you a bracelet. Or a band for your pretty hair."

"He's not my husband," Dakota said, so quickly that Trent almost smiled.

The sparse brows lifted, giving no doubt that she'd witnessed more than enough of their clinch to lead her to that assumption. "Well, then," she said, gamely shifting her sales pitch, "ask your fiancé—"

"He's *not* my fiancé." Dakota rolled her eyes and grunted in frustration.

Time to seize control of the situation, he decided. "Thanks for the offer, ma'am, but we aren't interested." He moved to wind the glass up again before she could argue, but the bandanna-covered head was halfway in the window. The old woman took in their embarrassed faces, squinting, calculating. Then she muttered something he couldn't catch, and the thin hand was waving a single string of beads under his nose.

"Give this to the lady," she commanded. "Jumbie beads," she added, as if that meant something.

He was about to lose his patience. "Ma'am, I told you we aren't interested. Could you let us move on?" He revved the engine meaningfully.

"Take it," she insisted. "Give it to the lady." She gave Dakota a broad, uneven grin that seemed almost conspiratorial.

Trent decided to take the path of least resistance. With all the grace he could muster, he reached out and took the necklace from the scrawny fingers. "How much?"

She looked from Dakota's flushed face to his irritated one, and said confidently, "Ten dollars."

"*Ten* dollars?" he exploded. He gave the necklace a disdainful look. It was nothing but a length of fishing line, strung with shiny, egg-shaped red beads. Each bead had a large black dot at one end, giving him the eerie sensation that he was being stared down by several dozen eyes. The nylon string was knotted at random intervals, in no order that he could discern. In the middle of the contraption, a small, corkscrew-shaped shell dangled like a pendant. "This isn't worth—"

Dakota's frustration bubbled over, and she began fishing for her purse. "Either you pay her, Trent, or I will."

She was right; they both had work to do. Cutting Dakota off with a gesture, he quickly extracted a bill and handed it over. The woman stuffed it down her scrawny bosom, looking almost surprised that he'd given in. Then she crinkled her eyes at Dakota, and again, Trent had the impression she was sending a message in some feminine language that his high testosterone count prevented him from deciphering.

"Once he put it on you, don't take it off until you leave Tobago, okay, sugar plum?" the woman advised, in that too-young, floating-on-the-wind voice. Then she threw them both a happy grin and stepped away.

Trent waited until the woman disappeared in his rearview mirror before holding up the string of beads. "You really want this thing, or shall I toss it?"

She shrugged and half smiled. "Probably the only souvenir I'll get while I'm here."

He gave it a second look. It was rather pretty, if you ignored the sensation of being watched by the beads' tiny black eyes. He slipped it over her head and arranged it so the single brown and white shell in the middle settled between her breasts. "In that case, enjoy."

She stroked it absently, and to his surprise, was smiling up at him as if he'd handed her something in a small, Tiffany-blue box. "Thank you."

He nodded courteously, warmed by her smile, but unsettled by the wave of pleasure that ran through him at giving her a gift, even something so humble. His awareness that they were alone again, and the memory of what they'd been doing before they were interrupted by the strange old woman, came back with full force.

It must have for her, too. "Forgot where we were for a second." She laughed nervously.

He nodded, the invasion having sobered him up like a dip in the sea. He hated watching the passion he'd aroused leach from her eyes and cheeks. She belted herself in, and playtime was over. "Scarborough, then," she said determinedly.

"Scarborough," he agreed. Work to be done, careers to build, money to make. But why did he feel like he'd rather just sit on the sand with Dakota and stare out into the ocean?

Chapter 9

Excitement hung like a blanket over Immortelle Park, in an almost tangible mist of anticipation and activity. This time, even though the street in front was thronging with cars, Trent's pass got them waved through without a problem. As the gates to the main parking area opened to them, Dakota craned her neck, searching outside the windows for the group of boys from yesterday. Nothing. Maybe their security guard nemesis had succeeded in chasing them away. Maybe they'd found something else to do. She felt an unanticipated pang of disappointment.

He noticed her glance in the direction where they'd first seen them standing, and said sympathetically, "Maybe they found something else to do today."

By now, she'd learned not to be surprised when he spoke her thoughts. The ability seemed to come naturally to him. Once parked, he came around and helped her out, and as she stood beside him while he locked the door, she wondered how fast the casual, languorous warmth between them would dissipate. Since their kiss in the car, he'd kept his hand lightly on her knee, a signal of future intent, a declaration that he planned on keeping his promise to return to her bed before they left Tobago.

But they were on the battleground now. She was the huntress, searching for a good story, or any story that her readers would crave. He was the protector, arming himself and his clients against intrusion and the prying eyes of the scandal-hungry public. This is what it all boiled down to: his job was to protect his turf, and hers was to encroach upon it. Would their sexual afterglow survive that cold, harsh reality?

The warm, relaxed lines of his face settled into something sterner, and she had her answer. Her thoughts were his. When he touched her again, it was gracious rather than intimate. He offered her his arm as they crossed the grassy expanse between the parking lot and the concert tents. Gingerly, she took it.

The dress rehearsal was about to get started, but instead of heading to the main area, he led her backstage, where a guard closely examined their passes before letting them through. On the other side, Trent stopped.

"Full schedule?" he asked.

"Pretty much." She was cautious, noncommittal, but softened her reluctance with a smile.

"Got time to squeeze in a few more interviews?" When her mouth formed a puzzled *O,* he fished in his pocket and withdrew another of his business cards.

"You already—" she began.

"Got a pen?"

She passed it over, and he scribbled some numbers on

the back, then handed her both card and pen. "What's this?" she asked, puzzled.

"Private numbers for Mango Mojo and Ryan Balthazar. Call them and see if they can slot you in today." Then, he added, as if it needed clarification, "For an interview."

He was setting her up with two of his top acts? How? Why? "But you've banned them from talking to me."

"I never banned anyone. I told you."

"They've certainly never been down for an interview with me before," she persisted. "Their publicist barely gave me a 'no' before she slammed down the phone."

"I'm sure, but that was probably out of loyalty to me. It certainly wasn't under my orders."

She frowned at the card. As glad as she was for the connection, she certainly hadn't expected it. "Why would they see me now?"

"I asked them to," he said casually, as if a request from him was all it took for doors to be opened.

This was a great opportunity. Mango Mojo, the young boy band, were media whores who couldn't resist an interview, so the blogs and airwaves were saturated with their stories, but Ryan Balthazar was almost as reclusive as Trent himself, and an interview with him would be quite a coup. She should be ecstatic. Instead, she was suspicious. She'd been down this path before, and the consequences had been disastrous. "Why now?"

He looked as if he didn't quite understand, so she explained. "Would you have set me up with them even one day ago? Would you have let me talk to your people yesterday?"

He understood where she was coming from and

began to protest. "It's got nothing to do with what happened between us last night. Well, not exactly."

"Not *exactly?* What's that supposed to mean? One minute your team's off-limits. Then we spend a…a… night in bed…" She felt her neck get hot at the mention of their night of sweaty, skin-on-skin contact. "Then all of a sudden the gates to the castle are thrown open. I can only assume this is some sort of…bonus. Like a tip for sleeping with you."

He was incredulous. "A *tip?* I tip waitresses and doormen. I don't tip the women I sleep with."

She threw her hands in the air in sheer frustration. "So maybe *tip* is the wrong word. But are you giving me this in exchange for the sex? If you are, it's unethical. I'm a journalist." She looked at him directly. "I don't sleep with men for stories."

He looked as if this was the last conversation he wanted to be having, but reined in his impatience enough to answer, "I never asked you to trade sex for a story. I gave you those contacts of my own free will—"

"The morning after you jump my bones—"

"I hope you don't think that's all it was. I don't think I've even used that term since college."

A worker shuffled past them, carrying a barrel-shaped object that was way too heavy, grunting as he went. To assure their privacy, Trent bent forward and spoke into her ear. "And I'd like to think that sleeping with me is its own reward."

She jumped back, scandalized. "You arrogant—"

He laughed softly, and then took the hand that held the card, curving her fingers over it to make a fist. The sharp edges of the card pressed into her skin. "Take the numbers, Dakota. Do the interviews. Believe me, I gave them to you because I wanted to. Because in the past 24 hours, I got to know you better, and I think I can trust you with them. Okay? No strings attached. No… obligation implied."

She desperately wanted to accept his offer. There wouldn't be just one story here, but enough to keep her column busy for a few days. Maybe it wasn't so bad after all…. It was an opportunity any professional would not let pass. Mollified by his reassurances, she let her protests drop. "Well, okay."

He smiled down into her face. "You're welcome."

His infectious smile and dry humor made her lips curve. "Thank you. I—"

There was a noise, the sound of heavy feet, and a man appeared in an open doorway. The festival's musical director. He looked anxious, his dark face taut. "Mr. Walker! Thank God. I need to talk to you." He glanced in Dakota's direction for half a second, and then dismissed her—and the conversation she and Trent were having—as inconsequential. "It's important."

Trent's brows twitched as he recognized the urgency in the man's tone, and gave Dakota an apologetic glance. "Looks like I've got a few fires to put out."

She stepped away, breaking their connection. "It's okay. You go ahead and deal with whatever…"

He was already pulling away from her, his body angled in the direction of the impatient man. "We'll stay in touch by phone. I'll see you after the dress rehearsal."

She nodded, understanding perfectly, but still feeling bereft. "Sure." Before she could add, "See you," Trent was gone.

A little past noon, Dakota stepped out of Ryan Balthazar's dressing room, pleased with herself. The interview had gone well. Instead of the cold wall of silence that had surrounded him and his publicist, the urbane soul singer was warm and talkative. He gave a great interview, even opening up enough to share some stories about his youth that Dakota didn't remember seeing published anywhere. She was gleeful at having an exclusive.

Ryan stood at the door of his tiny room, holding it open for her, shifting his body to allow her to pass, as if his 98-pound frame was any impediment. He looked like he'd stepped out of a Walter Mosley novel: thin, very dark, his long hair permed and held back in a glossy ponytail, a scrawny moustache and soul patch struggling to grow on his face. His shirt was peacock-bright, his pants well tailored. Anyone looking at him would immediately discount him as the class nerd... until they heard the soul-stirring, panty-dampening Barry White voice that boomed from his skinny chest.

As Dakota passed him, he accidentally-on-purpose brushed against her arm. He was a ladies' man, in spite of his slight stature. He'd been dripping honey over her from the moment she'd walked into his room, in that way some men did when they felt that if they made a pass at every female in their vicinity, it was a mathe-matical certainty that they'd bed at least a few.

"Thanks again," Dakota said, clutching her voice re-corder as if it held a treasure. "I can't wait to get work-ing on this. I'm so glad you agreed to see me."

"No problem," he answered in a voice like smooth thunder. "Any friend of Trent's is a friend of mine." He gave her a slow, lazy once-over that almost made Da-kota laugh. She had news for him; her sexual needs had been well taken care of the night before, and by someone who had a hundred pounds on Ryan, and a few other delightful physical attributes besides.

Instinctively, her hand came up to touch the pretty, strange little beads Trent had placed around her neck, an unspoken promise to make her a willing participant in another steamy session as soon as possible. Outside, she kept her composure. Inside, she was grinning like an idiot. Ryan and his Barry White boom would have to take a backseat.

She stepped into the corridor, trying hard to ignore Ryan's blatantly admiring look. Sounds from the dress rehearsal penetrated backstage, slightly muffled, but still stirring up a whirlpool of anticipation in her. The music world; this was what she lived for. The sound, the smell, the excitement. She looked at her watch. She had more than fifteen minutes before her next appointment. Maybe she could slip around to the front of the stage and see who was performing.

A slamming door jolted the thought from her head. She jumped at the vehemence of it, spinning around in time to see Trent and another man emerge from a dressing room two doors down. Dakota recognized Shanique's manager, Enrique. The grossly overweight man, his cheeks magenta from the tropical heat and crisscrossed with broken capillaries, panted to keep up with Trent. His white shirt was drenched with dark perspiration stains. He looked none too happy.

Neither did Trent. "If you can't do something about it," he barked at the poor man, "I will."

"I'm sorry," Enrique puffed.

"You should have called me. What's wrong with all of you? Can't you see how important this is?"

Trent caught sight of Dakota, and stopped abruptly.

The fat man behind him skated to a halt just in time. Enrique spotted Dakota, too, and a look of disdainful recognition crossed his red, blotchy face. His tiny eyes drew in to a hostile squint. Trent might have been willing to set aside the circumstances behind Shanique's downfall, but her manager certainly wasn't.

"What happened?" Dakota asked. The reporter in her had all her senses afire. The expression on Trent's face was one she hadn't seen before; a mixture of anxiety, irritation, weariness and concern.

And then the expression was gone, wiped clean like a scribbled secret on a whiteboard. It was replaced by a cautious alertness. His lips drew taut. "Just something I need to deal with," he answered evasively.

Hovering in the doorway, Ryan asked over Dakota's head. "Isn't she here yet?"

Dakota turned her head toward the question, her built-in, story-alert system beeping like crazy. "Isn't who here yet?" she asked, but the question didn't need to be answered. Shanique had missed dress rehearsal. Dakota knew that in the show-biz world, missing rehearsal was nothing short of a catastrophe. The question was…why?

Ryan, who wouldn't know a delicate situation if it smacked him in the face, went on. "I knew it. I saw it in her eyes. And after yesterday—"

Tight-lipped, Trent gave Ryan a single, cutting look. It was like a puff of air extinguishing a candle. Ryan was instantly sheepish, the lazy flirtatiousness toward Dakota gone. He began to babble, trying his best to recover from his gaffe. "Maybe she went to the beach and forgot the time. Maybe she's out with her crew, buying…T-shirts and shells and stuff."

He trailed off miserably, and then decided it was time to get the heck out of the firing zone. He bowed—actually *bowed*—in Dakota's direction. With a hurried, "It was a pleasure, ma'am," he pulled his head in between his shoulders like a turtle retreating inside its shell, and backed into his room. The door shut with a hasty click.

Dakota felt her breathing quicken. The air between her and Trent was thick and hot, and she knew without asking that Shanique wasn't here because she was in no condition to be. It could only mean one thing: his diva was off the wagon. She remembered how the singer had tripped over a wayward electrical cord onstage last evening, as she was charging toward the edge to berate Dakota. Even her tirade and sense of personal persecution had been over the top. Dakota should have suspected, but maybe she'd been blinded or distracted by other factors, namely Trent's proximity and Shanique's jealousy at the fact that Dakota and Trent were staying at the same resort. A jealousy, as it turned out, that was well-founded.

What was going on with Shanique? Was she drunk? High? Both? "Do you know where she is?" she asked Trent.

He looked as if he was weighing the pros and cons of answering even such a simple question, but eventually admitted, "She's on her boat. I'm going there now."

Dakota had heard that Shanique had opted not to use a hotel while in Tobago, but instead was staying on a luxury yacht moored at a nearby beach. "Do you want me to come with you?"

Trent's look of stark incredulity and his abrupt, "No," were overlaid by a snort of contempt from Shanique's manager. "Sure, Walker. Let the fox into the henhouse, why don't ya? Why not let this…hack take another swipe at Shanique and ruin us all?" His face was so curdled with disgust and loathing that Dakota half expected him to spit on the floor.

She stepped back, her spine rigid, stung not by the obnoxious man's blithering, but by Trent's one-word dismissal. She searched his face, trying to find a shred of regret for his tone or his harsh rejection, but saw only a mask of neutrality, and that stung even worse. This man might be willing to heat her up between the sheets, but he really didn't trust her professionally.

She began to back away. "Very well. I guess you'll be gone for the rest of the day?"

He shrugged, but didn't answer.

"Don't worry about me," she began—as if he'd be worried! "I'll finish up here and take a cab back to the…" She was about to say "cabin" but the last thing she wanted was for the pig-eyed man glowering at them both to know that she and Trent were sharing accommodations, never mind a bed. "…resort," she finished lamely.

He nodded. "Fine." And there it was: a flicker of regret, but it was gone almost before Dakota could let it sink in. He turned, and Enrique spun to follow him, but not before sending a final, dagger-pointed glare in Dakota's direction. The men retreated into the room they had just left, and the second the door slammed shut, the yelling began anew.

Dakota realized she was still clutching the voice recorder in her sweaty palm. She dried it carefully, slipped it into her bag and made her dizzy way to the main area. A jazz duo from the Cayman Islands was belting out a smoky melody, but she didn't stop to listen. She had another interview scheduled in just a few minutes, and her stomach wouldn't sit still.

She tried to get the look in Trent's eyes and the curtness in his voice out of her head, but couldn't. Just like that, they were back in their old roles. She was the nosy—and dangerously astute—journalist, and he was the man with secrets to protect and a reputation to maintain. She was a threat to his business, and especially, his precious singer.

With a pang, she wondered just how much of Trent's concern for Shanique was due to his position as her producer, and how much of it came from the fact that he'd once been her lover. Trent had told her their affair was all in the past, but how was she to know for sure? It was obvious he still hadn't fully sorted out his feelings for her. Just how deep did those feelings go, and how far would he go to protect the woman he once loved?

Chapter 10

The question of Trent's loyalty—and attachment—to Shanique took root in Dakota's mind and began to grow, like one of those alien spores on the science fiction channel. By nightfall, back at Rapture once more, she had almost completely given herself over to the idea; images of Trent and Shanique whirled in her mind. Shanique was on a bender, with one day to go to her comeback concert. Trent was trying to soothe her, reason with her, plead with her to come to her senses and sober up enough to go onstage. And Shanique would be clinging to him, all six feet of her, feminine and beautiful, a damsel in distress. Trent was a sucker for women who needed to be rescued. The way he'd given her a roof over her head when she most needed it had taught her that about him.

Dakota tried to focus on her laptop screen as she sat on the patio. She finished two columns, and with a few clicks, sent them zooming through the ether to her editor. Usually, when she finished a good article, she felt a sense of satisfaction, a calm after the storm of writing. But tonight, she felt unsettled and dissatisfied. She felt alone.

She shut down her computer, slipped it into its case and then rose to gather up the remains of her dinner. She'd opted to eat at the cabin, rather than subject herself to whatever shenanigans were going on in the main hall. She was in no mood for naked mah-jongg or pornstar trivia or whatever Declan had dreamed up for his guests tonight. Floating around on her lonesome amidst a sea of happy couples? No, thank you.

She heard a crunch of gravel on the path and recognized the solid, determined footfalls. Holding her plate in one hand and her glass in the other, she watched as Trent appeared from around a pink oleander. His normally straight shoulders were curved under a burden of fatigue, but the second he saw her, he brightened and straightened up.

"Hey," he said, and the creases around his mouth deepened in a smile.

"Hi," she responded, but she wasn't smiling. She watched him approach, her body stiffening. She was vaguely aware that if she clutched her glass any harder it would crack in her hand. She was still galled by his dismissal and still burning from his unguarded mistrust. And yet he was smiling, glad to see her. As if coming home and finding her waiting for him made everything all right.

He stepped onto the patio, feet echoing heavily on the wood. Slowly, almost carelessly, he bent toward her, and as he moved she could detect his warm scent, mingling with the flowers that were filling the evening air with their fragrance.

Something leaped inside her, a gladness. It was so good to see him; it felt almost domestic, waiting for her lover to come back to her after a long day's work.

Then she remembered where he'd been, and why she hadn't been with him. She was not going to yelp in happy welcome like a puppy whose master had returned. He'd cut her cold back at the festival site, made it all too evident that she wasn't welcome to share in his business affairs. It was dumb, she knew. He had every right to protect his acts, and to set up barriers of protection around them if he needed to. But as much as she'd tried to convince herself that the attraction between her and Trent was purely physical, a childish, irrational part of her was hurt.

She pulled away, and his kiss fell on dead air. His look of surprise was almost comical.

She whirled around and headed for the kitchenette, where she began washing up her dishes. It gave her an excuse not to look at him…because catching his eyes might make her weaken.

He followed and stood off to her right, leaning against the countertop, arms folded. The tingle at her neck told her his eyes never left her. She stacked away the plate, glass and cutlery, and dried her hands. Now what?

"I know there aren't any prizes for stating the obvious, but you're angry."

"No," she denied sulkily. "I am not—"

He grasped her by the arms, making sure she couldn't make a run for it. "I'm sorry."

"For what?" she asked. She had so many reasons

to be mad at him. Which one, if any, was he apologizing for?

"For being so short with you today. I'm sorry, but I was worried."

"What were you worried about?" she probed.

His face tautened. "You know I can't get into that."

Her anger calcified, with hard, spiky edges. "Because you don't trust me."

His only reaction was a twitching muscle in his jaw. "Protecting her is part of my job."

"Protecting her from snoops like me," Dakota said, unable to keep the hostility out of her voice.

He slumped. "That's not what I meant."

"It's what it felt like." Exhaustion tumbled down upon her. She longed to crawl into bed, never mind that she hadn't had a shower yet. But Trent was standing between her and the bedroom. He seemed to be taking up more space than he should, filling up the narrow doorway. She was too proud to ask him to let her by.

His face was creased and weary, and she wondered for the first time if he'd had anything to eat, or if he'd rushed back to the cabin…to see her. She felt petty and ashamed.

"Let's not fight," he suggested. "Please." He was visibly trying to push away the stresses of the day. "Can we agree to leave our…professional differences…outside the cabin door? Can we forget about our business lives when we're alone together…in here?"

"You mean—" she licked her lips "—there's a daytime you and me, who go about our business and stay out of each other's way, and a nighttime us who…" She stopped, blushing like crazy. "Who can be…"

"Lovers," he suggested. He was standing too damn close for comfort.

"We're not in love," she hastened to remind him.

He smiled, indulging her denials. "Bedmates, then." His anger had completely dissipated, his voice seductive, warm and inviting. "Adventurers. Explorers of all Rapture has to offer."

He was making her nervous…and hot. "You think that's it? The *resort* is doing this to us?" Her fingers flew up to the red-and-black bead necklace at her throat. It felt warm to her touch.

"I don't know about you," was his silky response, "but Rapture and all its toys and love lotions and games can go to hell. *You* are doing this to *me*." He closed the gap between them, in part by stepping closer, in part by pulling her to him. Their mouths collided. Not in the sensual, languorous, post-sex way they had this morning in the car, but urgently. It was as if kissing her had been the carrot he'd been dangling before himself all day.

Instantly, her body was aflame, like a match to paper. The heat of her ire was transformed into a different kind of heat. His hands were on her waist, holding her against him, but they dropped to her bottom, grasping each firm, full globe with obvious appreciation. She'd changed out of her jeans and into a short cotton dress, and the fabric was no barrier against the warmth of his skin.

He, on the other hand, was still in the polo he'd left in that morning, and the day's stress and exertion had left him smelling of dust, grime, and sea salt. The effect was intensely masculine, even animalistic. She pulled her mouth away from his and buried her face in his neck to draw in his scent, getting instantly drunk off it.

"God, you smell good," she groaned against his throat. The sprouting stubble at his chin scraped her cheek, and she loved the sensation.

He laughed softly. "I smell like wild game." Insistently, he yanked up the hem of her dress, exposing her from the waist down, running his fingertips along the line where the top of her panties met her bare belly. The intense shock of the contact made her want to scream. "I should take a shower," he murmured, but made no effort to let her go.

"Don't you dare." Caution and decorum were blown away. Her resentment completely gone. In their place was wanton lust. She shamelessly held her hand out between them, flat against the button fly of his jeans, which was stretching forward to meet her halfway. The ridge under the denim was an open invitation…and she was ready to accept. "I like you like this."

"You're kidding."

"No, really." She ran her tongue against the line of his jaw, making him groan. "You could be my wild man tonight. We could do it on the floor." The sex spirits that roamed the gardens and cabins of Rapture had taken full possession of her body, and she was reckless, hungry beyond belief. "We could do it on the porch. Under the samaan tree. I want to smell you." The rational remnant of her mind was listening, shocked at her admission of desire; the part of her mind overrun with lust drowned out the feeble protest. "I want you to cover me with—"

She choked in midsentence, silenced by the sudden whiff of an odor that wasn't Trent's. It wasn't sweat, wasn't testosterone, wasn't salty Tobago air. It was perfume. A woman's perfume; heavy, expensive, oppressive. It was the kind Dakota wouldn't be caught dead wearing.

It was, however, the kind Shanique was paid big bucks for endorsing…and swore she wore every day.

Dakota shot out of Trent's arms, wriggling from his grasp so suddenly she fell over, banging the same elbow she'd smashed in the dark the night before. She yelped in pain, and instantly, he was on his knees beside her. "Are you okay? What happened?"

His hands were on her, concerned this time, helping her up, but she grasped them and thrust them off her. Rage was ablaze in her. "Don't touch me!" she snarled.

If the situation weren't so dire, his confused expression would have made her laugh. "I don't understand.…"

She got up, smoothing down her bunched skirt, furious with herself for having let him lift it in the first place. Embarrassed at having lost her balance. Ashamed at her brazen, wanton come-on. "What's there to understand?"

He folded his arms, frowning. "Forgive me if I'm a little perplexed. Ten seconds ago you were begging for it—"

"Don't be vulgar!"

He acknowledged his mistake with a stiff incline of the head. "I'm sorry. But I thought you…wanted…you and I…" He waved his hands in frustration at being unable to express himself, and ended with, "What happened?"

"Maybe," she said bitingly, "you should have taken that shower *before* you got here."

Her comment didn't alleviate his confusion in the

least. "What? Look, Dakota, I've been out all day. I'm quite sure I stink. I can hit the shower now, and be out in ten. Then we can pick up where we—"

"Like hell." She darted past him and headed for the bedroom, anxious to get away. Hating the conversation she didn't want to have. He was hot on her tail, anger and rejection joining his puzzlement. Before she could find refuge in her room, he grabbed her by the arm and spun her around.

"What the hell just happened? Can't you at least tell me that much?"

"What happened," she said scathingly, "is that you got more perfume on you than a counter girl at a department store!"

He stared at her for several seconds and then gingerly pulled the collar of his polo up to his nose and sniffed. His brows lifted as he processed the scent, and then he let his shirt collar go. "Shanique's, I guess," he said dismissively.

She slapped her forehead in feigned astonishment. "No, really?"

It took him long enough, but he finally understood. "Sugar, you don't think—"

"Don't *sugar* me! And what I think is obvious!"

"What you think is wrong," he said firmly. "I put my arms around her."

"Why?"

"She was upset," he answered, as if that was obvious. "Her comeback's tomorrow. She's not sure she can hack it. She was hysterical." His top teeth clamped down on his lower lip, as if he feared he'd said too much to the journalist in her. But the journalist in her didn't give a crap about Shanique's condition. The woman in her...

well, that was another story. "So you *comforted* her," she filled in bitterly.

"Not in the way you obviously think. I held her. That was all."

"Sure. And how long did you *hold* her?"

"As long as I needed to. Until she stopped crying."

"Like a lover."

"Like a friend." He sucked his teeth in irritation, turned sharply as if retreating up the corridor in disgust, and then spun to face her just as sharply, when part of him that wanted to stay and talk took over the reins. "Listen to me. My relationship with Shanique ended a long time ago. It's finished. She works for me. So if you're going to let jealousy eat you up every time she and I—"

"I am not jealous!" To her ears, her voice was shrill.

"What are you, then?" he challenged.

Dakota searched for words. "Disgusted. Offended."

"Offended?"

"That you would leave one woman's arms and come to me—"

"Oh, for Pete's sake," he groaned. "If you don't want to explore this…thing…between us…" He paused, and let his gaze run over her flushed face and down her trembling body. "If you want to call it quits, I won't press you. But I think we've got something.…"

The look he gave her made her shiver even harder. *I think we've got something, too,* she wanted to tell him but her throat was glued shut. She couldn't get into another relationship with a music mogul. She couldn't afford to have her heart devastated by one more powerful, wealthy…

He went on. "If you're such a coward that you'd grasp

at a straw just so you don't have to deal with the feelings you're having for me…fine."

Deny, deny! a voice inside her said. Instead, she stayed silent.

"But don't reduce me to less than I am. I am no liar, and I am no cheat." His anger was like a pillar of fire. His face was so close to hers she could feel his breath.

Then he put space between them. She watched his stiff back until he disappeared into the smaller bedroom. He didn't exactly slam the door, but the decisive click left no doubt that the conversation was closed for the night.

She opened her bedroom door, but stood there indecisively. She longed to run to his door and bang on it until he opened up. She wanted to yell an apology through the keyhole; but no words came. She'd offended him, hurt him, even. Jealousy had turned her into an idiot.

What had she done? If she'd managed to keep hold of her emotions, she could have been with him now. Naked, on the floor like she'd teased. Panting, delirious. She tingled at the memory of the invitation she'd tossed to him. *Let's do it on the porch. Under the huge tree in the garden. Let Rapture sweep us away.*

Instead, she was sleeping in an empty bed, dealing with the guilt of having hurt the man who'd only wanted to make her feel good. A man she was coming to care for. She stepped inside, let the door close, and leaned heavily against it. *Great job, Dakota,* she chided miserably. *Proud of yourself?*

Chapter 11

The only word Dakota could think of was *magic*. It was so cliché she almost felt embarrassed, but there was something about the perfection of the evening that almost made her believe in the supernatural. The sky above was perfectly black, and scattered with a billion stars, like a painted canopy pierced by diamond-bright points of light. From the nearby sea came the crisp scent of salt, sand and seaweed. She closed her eyes and imagined the small wooden boats moored close to shore for the night, bobbing on the black water.

Under her feet, springy grass gave way as she walked, their blades bruised by hundreds of pairs of feet, adding another layer of scent to the already aromatic air. The heat of the spectators' bodies rose around her, filling the tents, made bearable only by the ocean breeze. And the music… Oh, the music was sublime. Earthy jazz poured down from the stage, guitars weeping, saxophones wailing, trumpets, trombones, horns, joining in a collective moan like a woman being pleasured in bed. The evening would have been perfect.

If only her chest didn't ache as if a rock was lodged at the center of it.

She stood among the large crowd at the opening night of the Jazz festival, feeling more alone than she could ever remember. She might as well have been stranded on a rock, watching people party aboard a passing ship and knowing they could neither see nor hear her.

All day, she'd been alone in the cabin. She was supposed to be writing up stories, but couldn't focus long enough to get her thoughts in sequence, much less write them down. The utter stillness of the room had been almost suffocating. Trent had been gone when she woke up that morning, and she wasn't surprised. It was a busy day for him and his performers; it was his job to be at their side. She tried to convince herself that the fight they'd had last night had nothing to do with his leaving without talking to her.

Nevertheless, she'd obsessively checked her phone for messages and willed herself not to rush blindly down to the festival venue to see if he was there (of course he was) and who he was talking to (his performers, who else?). But although she stayed back at the cabin specifically to get some work done, she'd just sat before her laptop, scowling. When she left for the festival, the cursor was still at the top of a blank page, blinking.

She shivered, in spite of the heat. A reaction to the intense ripples of emotion that rolled through her every time she thought of Trent. It was crazy, this mishmash of feelings; desire and curiosity, jealousy and anger, trust, mistrust. She laughed softly to herself. It was like the callaloo soup she'd had on her first night in Tobago: a swirling pot of everything, chopped up and whipped together, until she could hardly identify a single ingredient.

Tingles went up and down her spine, making the fine hairs on her arms move like a field of wheat in a gentle breeze, but not because of Trent. Shanique had begun singing on the main stage. Her voice was that of a fallen angel, so sweetly perfect that the sea of people gathered around were captive under her spell. Her song was haunting, urgent and vulnerable. It was as if she gave voice to the turmoil that had enveloped Dakota since she'd landed.

And the voice, she was certain, was Shanique's. No lip-synching here. Trent would never have allowed it, anyway. The demons the songstress had been battling yesterday were sleeping. Whatever Trent had said or done while he'd held her—Dakota forced the image out of her fraught imagination—had worked. Shanique was glorious.

And, near the edge of the stage, Trent was watching, arms folded across his chest, his face a study in concentration. He was in a charcoal gray suit, despite the humidity, looking serious, professional and reserved. She watched as he turned his head in her direction.

Her body went rigid, as if by not moving she would fade from his field of vision, and his brow-shrouded gaze would pass over her. No dice. It was as if he'd spotted her long before, and knew exactly where to find her. With great purpose, he turned from the stage and headed in her direction.

Dakota fought the urge to smooth her hair and her dress, but she could do nothing about the moisture gathering in the corners of her eyes. With chagrin, she realized that Shanique's song had brought her to the brink of tears.

A warm pillar was at her side, a voice in her ear. "Beautiful, isn't it?"

Somehow Trent appeared right next to her. She jumped, and her heartbeat skated off the charts. She knew at once what he was talking about; that undeniable, haunting voice. "And to think I almost…" She stopped. To think her story had brought low such a talent, almost destroyed such a star. She felt rotten. The standard journalistic excuse, the people's right to know, felt hollow and insubstantial. She hadn't written that story because of anyone's *right to know.* She'd written it because it would have been a shot in the arm for her career. The fallout for Trent and anyone else be damned. Shame made her throat burn.

Trent, unerringly as always, understood. His mouth was still close to her ear, and she longed for him to touch her, but he didn't. But what he said was worth even more. "You didn't destroy her, Dakota. You gave her a reason to save herself."

She swung her startled gaze in his direction. "You made it perfectly clear how you felt about what I did."

He nodded, dragging his eyes back from the stage to hold her stare. "And I meant it. You hurt her, me and a few others. But some people only feel the need to change direction, and rise again, after they hit rock bottom. And you made that happen."

She let that settle in her mind, like cloudy sediment in a bottle. "Thanks…I guess."

Amazingly, he smiled, and that made all the difference. The jumble of emotions that had been jostling

inside her all evening became still. Anger, hurt and
resentment flew from her, like spirits cast out, leaving
only a burning desire for him to hold her, right here,
amidst the packed concert audience, and dance with
her to Shanique's exquisite song. Unable to stop herself, she smiled back.

The song ended and the applause was thunderous,
like storm clouds bursting. Shanique drank it in, arms
open as if she wanted to draw every man and woman in
the audience into her embrace. A halo glowed around
her dark face, like a moon in eclipse. "Thank you, thank
you," she began, modestly waving away calls for an en-
core. "I love you! Listen to me…listen!"

Her appreciative audience simmered down, eager to
hear what she had to say. She began a gracious comeback speech but it soon slid into tearful apologies for
her many mistakes, and declarations of love and appreciation for her loyal fans.

Trent looked at his watch, but Dakota didn't need
to glance at hers to know the diva was overstaying her
allotted time. Shanique was the top-billed act, closing
the show, and the concert was overdue to end for the
night. Fortunately, jazz was a fluid thing, and her audience didn't seem to mind. In fact, they were lapping it
up. Shanique was in a trance, swaying, arms still open,
pouring out her stream of consciousness to her eager
fans. "Most of all," she was saying, "I want to thank my
producer, Trent Walker, for always being at my side. For
being my friend. More than my friend. Trent, Trent, I
love you, I love you. I never stopped…"

The audience screamed in delight.

And the candle inside Dakota blew out.

Shanique turned this way and that, confused, searching. "Trent? Trent? Where are you?" A note of panic. Blinded by the lamps overhead. "I love you! Did you hear me?"

A large figure stepped onstage, florid face perspiring under the hot lights. It was Enrique, Shanique's manager. Dakota exhaled in relief as the man gently slipped an arm around Shanique's waist and led her away from the stage. The excited roar of the crowd followed her as she waved and blew kisses until she was out of sight.

Dakota sneaked a look at Trent. His face was like Stonehenge. "Is she...?" She was afraid to ask.

"Sober as a judge," he said shortly. "I made sure of it."

"Then why...?"

He shook his head. "A little overemotional, maybe. She was terrified of coming onstage tonight. She wasn't sure she could do it."

"She was fantastic," Dakota said honestly.

"She was. I guess she got carried away in the spirit of the moment."

Did she ever, Dakota thought, but was too smart to say. "Shouldn't you go to her? She was...uh...calling for you." *And declaring her undying passion,* she could have added, but didn't like how the thought made her stomach feel. And she knew if she said it, there'd be more emotion in her voice than she cared to reveal. She steeled herself for being left alone, but to her immense surprise, he shook his head vehemently.

"My being there would probably do more harm than good." The MC had taken the stage, and begun his farewells, directing the still jazz-hungry audience to the exits, promising them there was more in store for them the following night. But Trent's eyes were on the wings through which his singer had exited. "Her people will take care of her," he said decisively. He turned to look at her, abruptly, as if he'd slammed shut a door in his mind that led backstage. He was all hers again.

Her relief was tinged with a smidgen of shame; she wasn't the type of woman to get into a tug-of-war over a man. With everything in her heart, she wanted to believe him when he said it was over between him and the songstress. He'd sworn it, again and again, and his behavior tonight, his decision not to become embroiled in Shanique's drama, was ample evidence. He was right; Shanique's people would take care of her. He'd done all he needed to yesterday, reining her in just enough to get her onstage.

Dakota had given him hell for it. The only fair thing to do was apologize. "I know yesterday was rough on you."

He nodded in silent agreement.

"And I didn't make it any easier."

"No," he answered wryly. "You didn't."

She searched his face for evidence of leftover resentment or anger, but there was none. On the other hand, he wasn't exactly moving to bridge the gap between them. He was leaving that up to her.

She stretched her arm out—despite a sudden attack of muscle weakness—and touched him on the arm. "Trent? I was out of line. I'm sorry."

She felt him relax under her touch. "It's… Oh, I'll live." He gave her a half smile. "The expedition to the samaan tree would have been a first for me, though."

Her body went crazy hot at the memory of her daring him to take her under the huge tree and then, well, *take* her. "It's still there," she dared to say. And shivered in erotic anticipation.

His brows drew together. "You cold?" he asked in surprise, looking up at the bands of dark Caribbean sky visible in the spaces between the tents. He began taking off his jacket, but she waved it away with an embarrassed chuckle.

"No, of course not. Just someone walking on my grave, that's all."

He draped it around her shoulders anyway. Then, not removing his arm from around her, begin to guide her toward the exit. "Ready?" he asked, and gave her that slow, lazy smile that told her he wasn't just talking about leaving the festival.

I don't know, she asked herself. *Am I?*

When they arrived at Rapture, Declan was standing near the entrance to the main building. His dark skin made him almost disappear into the shadows, and his lightweight beige suit was ghostly. As they drew closer, Dakota noticed he was holding the huge iguana in his arms, stroking it like a movie villain with a cat. She flinched unconsciously. Trent was close enough to her to feel her reaction and gave her a comforting smile.

"Trent, Dakota, good evening. How was Jazz?" Declan's voice was a melody.

"Wonderful," Trent said pleasantly. "You couldn't make it tonight?"

Declan shook his head. The iguana reacted to the movement, scrolling his eyes outward to get a bead on whoever its master was talking to. Instinctively, Dakota raised a protective hand to her hair. "Anke went with a friend," he told them, "so I stayed back and held down

the fort. She should be here any minute now. I just want
to make sure she's back safe before I turn in."

As Dakota and Trent headed around the garden path
toward their cabin, rather than through the main hall,
Declan fell into step with them, casually cradling his
reptile like a father with a newborn. It protested the
movement by squirming, and with a chuckle he bent
over and released it. Dakota inflicted a few sharp nail
imprints on Trent's wrist as the monster scurried past
her and into the bushes.

At the sound of her gasp, Declan turned his head to
her. "If you think he's scary, imagine his ancestors."

"I'd rather not," she countered, and laughed. She
couldn't help liking their incredibly handsome, soft-
spoken, and good-natured host. As he smiled back, his
liquid molasses eyes happened to fall upon the thin
red-and-black necklace dangling between her breasts,
and his smile grew even broader. "You've really been
delving into the local culture, haven't you?"

Dakota's hand shot up to clutch the shell pendant.
"What? You mean this?"

He nodded in amusement. "Jumbie beads," he said
significantly.

"That's what the old lady said. What's so special
about jumbie beads?"

"*Jumbie* is a local term for a spirit, good or bad. People say these beads are magical. They attract spirits."

Dakota wasn't sure she liked the sound of that.

Declan gave her a reassuring smile. "I wouldn't be
too worried if I were you. But maybe if I had a closer
look, I could..." He gestured, and under the pale garden floodlights, began leaning forward to scrutinize
the necklace.

Dakota felt Trent stiffen beside her and was startled by his protective response to the idea of another man invading her personal space. She wondered if she should be charmed or alarmed.

Declan's dark head drew near, and with one long finger, he lifted the beads gently, humming softly to himself. When he straightened, his smile was reassuring. "Haven't seen one of those in a while," he commented.

"One of what?" Trent asked.

"Well, the psychological aspects of love and sex are really my specialty. I leave the metaphysical part to Anke. But I'd say what you have here is some sort of love charm." He indicated the seemingly random knots in the string. "Those knots are called bindings. They create soul ties between a woman—" the look he gave Trent was all-knowing "—and the man who gave them to her. And the shell, if I'm not mistaken, means you get one wish."

Just one, Dakota thought dryly. *Why not three, while we're at it?*

Trent's laugh was an abrupt, dismissive bark. "Tell me you don't believe in this nonsense."

Declan shrugged. "I was born here. Like every Tobagonian, I have moments when the most bizarre story seems...plausible."

"It's just a bit of fishing line and some dried beans," Trent insisted.

Dakota wasn't as quick to dismiss the idea, at least not all of it. There was more than one way in which a woman could be bound to a man, and the act of physical connection was first in her mind. Dakota was suddenly swamped by a flood of warmth that began around her neck and rolled downward in waves, to her nipples, around her belly button and over the bump of her belly to the smaller, snugger bump below.

The sensation was shoved aside by the more personal kind of binding. The emotional kind. The romantic kind. And on *that* one, she was with Trent. Magic beads? Binding knots? Ridiculous.

"Some old woman on the beach practically browbeat me into shelling out ten bucks for it," Trent insisted. "Doesn't mean a beanstalk will grow if we plant them."

Declan gave him the smooth, placating smile of a trained psychologist. "Maybe not. Maybe they're just... pretty beads." He smacked his hands together, bringing the conversation to an end with a decisive clap. "And now, after a long day, I think I'll leave you to your...rest."

If Dakota's face got any hotter, it would ignite. The men shook hands, and Declan bowed formally to Dakota. Then, he turned away and disappeared into the shadows. She and Trent stood at the top of the path leading to their cabin, listening to the rustle of his feet on the grass. Apart from that, the only sounds surrounding them were those of the tropical night. Frogs that sang like birds. Crickets that should have been avoiding the frogs, but were instead giving their location away with loud chirps. Even from where they stood, she could hear the tinkling of the wind chimes in their samaan tree as the breeze blew through it.

As they walked to their cabin, Dakota fingered her beads idly, reminding herself what a damn-fool, small-island load of bunk they were. She wanted Trent, and wanted him terribly, but that was all physical. It was lust, not magic. They alone were responsible for everything that went on between them.

Her emotions had been rubbed raw by the pure perfection of the jazz, which still coursed down over her
body like honeyed love oil. Not to mention the way
something inside of her was opening up to him. It was
as if he was unlocking a series of vaults, working away
at her like a patient locksmith. With every hour in his
presence, she was more and more open. To…what?

She stepped inside, and behind them, Trent shut the
door with a soft click, and faced her. His eyes were
searching. "You okay?"

"Tired." The word was nothing but an excuse, a de-
laying tactic. She was as nervous as a bride.

"Then let's have a shower—"

Something must have shown on her face, because he
added with amusement, "*Separate* showers, and meet
on the porch for drinks. How's that sound?"

He was being so gentle, it was obvious he knew
what was going through her head. Maybe it was going
through his, too. She was slipping into panic mode.
With Trent, what should have been just a little sexual distraction was in danger of becoming much more.
Emotions were coming into play. There was no way she
was allowing herself to be sucked into his personal vor-
tex. Not even trying to keep her voice steady, she said,
"Showers. Right." And darted down the hall.

The huge brass bed, which had been in damp disar-
ray from her troubled and sleepless night, was draped
in crisp, clean sheets. A small package, wrapped in a
lace doily, sat demurely atop each pillow as if the maid
assumed two people were sharing the bed. She examined one. It was homemade guava candy. She returned
it to its position, on the same pillow she'd sunk her teeth
into the night she and Trent had made love, to stop her-

self from screaming like an escapee from a mental asylum. The round-bellied, naked woman, still standing in her green river, looked down at her from the painting over the bed and smiled. *Go ahead, sister,* she seemed to say. *You know you want to.*

She stayed under the pounding water as long as she could, trying to ignore the memories of when she'd been fantasizing about a man she hadn't liked and didn't know, but who she'd come to like and know a whole lot more.

She dressed quickly, slapped a fresh bandage on the cut on her chin, and went out to the porch. Trent was dressed and waiting, his hair as damp as hers. He'd already opened a bottle of wine and poured them each a glass.

"You must have been a very dirty girl," he said silkily.

"Sorry I took so long. I…uh… The water just feels fantastic, doesn't it? And it tastes so sweet."

He offered her a glass. "And we both have a sweet tooth, don't we?"

If this was how it was going to be, she wouldn't be able to hold out until the wine was gone. But skillfully, discerningly, Trent led the conversation in a completely different direction, commenting on each performance with the casual expertise of a man who'd built his life on knowing and understanding music. She listened like a devotee at the altar of a guru, although she herself knew a thing or two about the industry. His opinions were almost visionary, and she wasn't so petty as to deny there was a lot he could teach her. When they'd finished their second glass, he set aside the wine and leaned forward, elbows on his knees, and speared her with a look.

She groaned silently. Was he going to suggest, in that dark-chocolate voice of his, that they proceed to her big brass bed, so he could make good on his promise-slash-threat? And when she accepted—because she knew she would—would he look into her eyes and know she was becoming sucked into him, drawn into a place where someone like her, who'd been burned by men in the music business before, had no place going?

His tongue left a wet trail across his lower lip, and he seemed to be enjoying watching her stretched out on tenterhooks. With a ghost of a smile, he asked, "Swim?"

Wait...what?

To fill her dumfounded silence, he laughed and said, "I was thinking of checking out the infamous pool."

"The nude pool?"

"The *clothing-optional* pool," he corrected humorously. "Join me?"

Thunder in her chest. The pool was nestled in a silent corner of the estate within a grove of orange trees. There was no doubt that in consenting to swim with him, she would be agreeing to more. In spite of her bravado, she knew that immersing herself into Trent Walker would be like stepping into quicksand.

"It's after midnight," she reminded him. If she hadn't still been seated, she'd have started backing away.

He shrugged. "I'm too keyed up to sleep. Aren't you?"

He had a point, but still, she resisted. "I'll probably just go for a walk." She waved her hand vaguely in every direction except the pool's.

"Alone? Want me to—"

"I'll be fine," she said hastily. "The estate's gated, remember?"

He looked about to argue but nodded slowly. "Cool. Enjoy it." He turned and walked toward the porch steps, still fully dressed in his polo and jeans.

"Aren't you going to get your swimsuit?" she called after him.

He threw a crooked smile over his shoulder. "I'm taking the other option." Then he was gone.

Chapter 12

The only way to chase the image of Trent swimming naked from her head was to embark upon a wretched walk she'd never intended to take in the first place. Stepping barefoot off the porch, she headed where he hadn't, moving off the stone path so she could enjoy the spiky grass between her toes. The moon had wandered off behind the clouds, leaving only a few curious stars to watch her.

As she walked, she set her hair free, and from time to time lifted her face to the sky as if the warmth of the sun still lingered there. But dammit, maybe her sense of direction was all screwed up, because twenty minutes later, she was standing at the edge of the orange grove. Beyond it, she could hear the sound of water lapping against the body of a lone swimmer.

Maybe her body knew exactly where it wanted to be, even if her mind didn't. Stepping through the trees was like falling through a sinkhole into an underground cavern. Green floodlights were placed low on the ground and sunken into the pool. The grass was thick and dotted with pink and lilac lilies. Nearer the pool's edge, flat gray stones were marbled with white.

The *pool* was no rectangular, chemical-blue hotel monstrosity. It was a grotto sunk in stone, surrounded in part by a half circle of rocks from which feathery ferns dangled. From the surface rose a fine mist resembling...steam?

Through the mist, a long brown arm rose and fell, followed by another, as Trent pulled himself lazily along. Even in the semidarkness, she could clearly see the broad triangle of his back gleaming in the water. The muscles tensed and relaxed as he swam, like they'd tensed and relaxed under her hands when they'd made love. She was sure he'd seen her, but instead of stopping, he went on with his laps, leaving in his wake a trail of bubbles that had pearled from his mouth and nose.

She took a few steps closer, green mist wrapping around her ankles, watching with intense fascination as he reached the end, jackknifed like a dolphin and— oh, my God, he really was naked.

His taut butt disappeared beneath the surface like a mythical beast in a loch, leaving her yearning for a second glimpse. Instead, there was an ominous ripple as he became one with the water—and headed her way.

He stood up in the water, rising in a cascade before her, eyes wide open as if he had been tracking her from below. Droplets fell from his long curly lashes, and as he wiped the water from his face, she realized she was as wet as he was—but not in the same way.

"Water's warm," he announced.

"Heated?"

He shook his head. "Nope. Hot spring. The pool fills from below." His tongue flicked against the mole on his lip, drawing her eyes to it. "Tastes of minerals. Sulfur and a couple others. Sulfur makes your skin glow, did you know?"

So does great sex, she thought. The gleam in his eye told her that was pretty much the message he'd hoped to send.

"Coming in?"

She glanced behind her at the silent grove, then back at him. She wasn't even going to use her lack of bathing suit as an excuse. Instead, she simply said, "I shouldn't."

He didn't argue. "I'm coming out, then." And to her delight and horror, he did. Venus rising from the sea might have been a sight, but Trent Walker emerging in all his naked splendor from a rock pool in sleepy Tobago would have made Botticelli drop his paintbrush. Water beaded in his hair and on his skin. It ran in tiny rivers among his chest hairs, to meet at his navel, and from there followed a single track downward. It took her gaze with it.

She could no more lift her eyes from his crotch than she could fully open them in the middle of dream sleep. He had to know she was staring, because in response, the thick, dripping column of flesh grew even thicker.

She wondered if she'd ever regain the power of speech.

As he towered over her, his hands were at her chin, nudging her face upward until she had no choice but to meet his gaze. "The human body's so much lighter in the water," he said, making her lust-tossed brain struggle to understand the significance. "I'd probably be able to lift you with one hand and settle you onto me. The other would be busy, though."

"Doing…what?" she croaked.

"Whatever you want." His lips were against her ear. "What *do* you want?"

She wanted something, that was for sure, or she'd have finished her walk and returned to her cabin like a good little girl. Want had conquered nervousness. Need had driven away doubt. Her desire for him had propelled her here, so to back down now would be ludicrous.

Her admission was torn from her like a confession at an inquisition. "Everything you can give me."

Her words of surrender hit home. Evidence of that was now jutting between her thighs. He whispered into her ear as if someone was listening from the trees. "I can give you plenty." Then she was in his arms and he was—no, he couldn't be—striding into the water with her like a sea monster dragging a maiden into the deep.

Not that the maiden was protesting.

She braced for contact with the water, but it was bath-warm. Her skirt ballooned, then clung to her hips as the fabric became soaked. As they descended shoulder-deep into the pool, the jumbie bead necklace also began to float.

"Take a deep breath," he instructed.

She never had the chance to ask why. He dunked her, then pulled her up again before the shock could register. Surprised laughter escaped her.

He grinned. "I wanted you to be nice and wet."

She had news for him: her body had already seen to that particular issue. Before she had a chance to say so, he was kissing her hungrily. She floated, steadied by his arms, thinking how right he was; in the water, she weighed nothing. The minerals on his water-slicked lips were a bittersweet aphrodisiac. The pungency of the sulfur tickled her nose, and something sweeter, which she couldn't identify, reminded her of the warmth with which he had flooded her mouth that night, when she'd tasted him for the first time.

She shivered, arching her back to look up at the sky. The moon was still AWOL. He nuzzled her neck, nipping at her collarbone with sharp teeth…and then he cursed.

"I think your bandage just floated away."

Her hand came up to gingerly touch her chin. "'S'okay. It's healing fast."

He dipped his head to take a look, and then agreed. "Looks good." He chuckled. "Clumsy, tripping around in the dark like that."

Incautiously, she answered, "My brain was fuzzy."

"Fuzzy brain? Not good. Why was it—"

She couldn't hold back her smile. "If only I could tell you."

He took her hand and brought it under the water, closing it around his thick hunk of hard, pulsing flesh. A reminder of what she could do to him—as if she needed one. "I'd say we were beyond secrets."

She hated the way he always made sense. They'd already crossed the boundaries of intimacy. Why not tell him the truth? The look on his face would be priceless. Slowly, she began stroking him, from base to tip, lightly, with just enough pressure to command his full attention.

"I was thinking about you."

"What…" He'd been holding his breath, she was certain, because he had to stop, inhale, and try again. "*What* about me?"

"Oh," she said with torturous casualness. "Just imagining what you'd be like in bed. Fantasizing the time away."

"Fantasizing about me?"

"Imagining you naked. Hard. Sexy. Like you are now." The pale underwater lighting was enough for her to see the outline of the flesh leaping in her hand. "Niiice," she appraised with heartfelt admiration.

He looked as pleased as if the organ she was stroking had won the blue ribbon for Best in Show. "Tell me what you were doing."

Her eyes took on a sly twinkle. "I could demonstrate, but it's hard to put on a show when you're neck-deep in water."

In a flash she was being carried aloft, until her bottom was braced against the rock face. Her skirt clung to her legs like wet leaves, but she peeled it away from her skin. With his eager help, she stripped off her panties. Exposed to him, and to the elements, some of her bravado slipped. "Don't let me fall," she begged.

"I'll catch you," he promised. And then, lest her mind stray, "Show me."

As the water cooled on the rest of her body, heat ramped up between her legs. She'd never done this in front of a man before. She'd let her mouth write a check, and her body had better be able to cash it. She slid her fingers down over her belly, and when they encountered heat and wetness, she sighed.

His hands cupped her butt cheeks, gently prying her apart so he could better see what she was doing. His gaze was riveted on her, face awestruck. Closing her eyes gave her courage; the gentle puffs of his excited breath against her reddening, tightening flesh made her wanton.

She moved her fingers in small, quick circles, too aroused to prolong the delicious agony, to taunt him like she'd planned. Her big exhibitionist debut should have been a drawn-out display that would allow her to flaunt her power over him, but Trent's excitement pushed her very far, very fast.

Her right hand came up to her lips while the other continued to do its job with practiced efficiency. Funny how she only used her left hand for *this*. She began sucking hungrily at her right thumb.

"You're giving me ideas," he grunted

It was giving *her* ideas. Her fingers flew faster, even faster, and her climax was like a lightning strike: confined to a small area, but devastating all the same. Before the pulse in her groin slowed, Trent hoisted her legs over his shoulders and began plundering her with his mouth with the savagery of a Caribbean pirate.

Orgasm hit a second time, without warning. The rocks under her bottom were sharp. The ferns tickled. But she could think of nothing but him, feel nothing but his mouth and the amazing, mind-numbing things he was doing to her.

When she opened her eyes again, the moon had come out of hiding.

"Cold?" Trent asked.

"You kidding?" she answered sleepily. "This is warmer than a Jacuzzi."

He smiled into her hair. He was standing shoulder-deep in the pool, enjoying the feel of Dakota's back against his chest. His arms were wrapped around her, and her breasts were lightweight against her forearms.

After her demonstration of dexterity—and shameless self-pleasure—he'd hauled her back into the water and made love to her with a ferocity that scared even him. It had been glorious; every nerve ending had responded to the stimulus of the warm water, cool breeze and her raw, throaty cries.

He was glad she didn't want to get out yet, but he'd thought he'd be a gentleman and ask.

"Who knew?" she murmured, almost to herself.

He was all over that one. "Who knew what?"

"That you'd be chivalry personified," she teased. "You're not nearly the butthead I thought you were."

He took her little barb with good grace. Although he still believed she'd once given him plenty reason to be nasty to her, things had changed, grown complicated. What could have been a few nights of tropical island sex was starting to feel like…more. She was smarter than he'd expected, and funny, passionate and deep. He discovered he didn't just want to sleep with her, he wanted to *know* her. The possibility that she just might let him was exhilarating.

He turned her around so he could look into her face. The water was just high enough to cover her nipples, but the mounds of flesh that it revealed made him think of bobbing for apples. He had to drag his mind back to what he wanted to say. "So, now that we've established I'm not the world's biggest butthead, do you think you'd be able to stand my company a little longer? After we get off the island?"

Her eyes searched his. "What do you mean?"

"I'm asking if you and I can see where this goes.

Beyond Rapture, with all of its games." He slid a finger deftly under the red-and-black necklace that stuck to her wet throat. "Far away from magic charms and the island air."

"You mean you want to see me after we get back to Santa Amata?"

He wished he could read her reaction, but he couldn't. "I don't want this to be a one-night stand or two-night stand, or anything you can count on your fingers—"

"I'm so sorry about that," she cut in. "I didn't mean—"

"I want to give it a chance to become what it is."

"What is it?" she whispered.

"What does it feel like for you?" he countered.

When she looked away, he felt a rush of excitement. It was proof that he wasn't the only one feeling what he was. There was something going on between them; that was for sure. They'd bonded in just a few short days. He didn't want to break that tenuous connection just yet.

The flash of doubt that crossed her face cut him to the quick. "We're too different," she hedged.

He slid one hand down over her bottom, partly to pull her against his naked body, and partly to prevent her from backing away, as his sixth sense told him she was a few seconds from doing. "Not that different. Or, at least," his voice lowered to a rasp, "the differences between us are mainly the good kind."

"You Tarzan, me Jane, huh?" she joked feebly.

"Something like that." Her resistance made him want to groan with frustration. He wasn't a vain man, but he knew he had a lot to offer. Women often threw themselves in his path, but he had gotten used to turning them down, not to being turned down himself. Rather than pique, he felt disappointment, and a vague sense of panic. Was Dakota really capable of spending time with him in Tobago, sharing hours of sweet, toe-curling sex with him, and then walking away the moment their plane landed in the States again? How cold-blooded was she?

But no, that wasn't it. Dakota's blood ran hotter than most. There must be another reason. He was going to get to the bottom of it if he had to pry it out of her. She felt the same yearning he did. He was sure of it.

She shut him out by closing her eyes, held her hand up to his chest as if warning him off. "It's no good." She sounded as if she was trying to convince herself, rather than him.

"It's very good," he contradicted her.

"I promised…" She spoke so softly, he shouldn't have been able to hear her, but his senses were sharpened by emotion and the clarity of the night air.

He pounced at once. "Promised who?"

"Myself."

"What did you promise yourself, sweetheart?" He tried not to sound too intense, so as not to scare her, but he had the agonizing feeling that so much hung on her response.

"That I wouldn't get involved with another man in the music business. The industry isn't kind to relationships. They don't last. It's the nature of the business. It's full of vain, self-absorbed people who don't mind using others to get what they want."

His incredulity must have shown on his face, because she hastened to back up her assertions. "Look at all the big stars, especially the ones that marry others in show business. One minute they're wrapped around each other, on the cover of every magazine, the next, they can't stand the sight of each other."

He got her point, but she was overreaching. What he and Dakota had…what he was beginning to believe they could have…had nothing to do with a bunch of spoiled, pampered musicians. "We aren't music stars. The kind of life they lead doesn't compare with ours."

"It goes all the way down the food chain," she insisted. "It's a disease that infects everyone. Show business makes you faithless and selfish and mean." The depth of her bitterness and hurt was apparent in her trembling lower lip. A bead of pool water clung to her lashes, and then rolled down her cheek.

Then, he understood. "Jeez, what did that guy do to you?"

"What guy?" she hedged.

"The one that messed you up. That one from last year." He felt an irrational, protective anger. He had no idea what had happened between her and this mysterious man, but whatever he'd done to her had caused some damage, and that was something he'd have to answer for. Trent wanted to be the one who made him answer.

"Isaiah didn't mess me up," she said hastily. Even now, he thought irritably, she was defending this guy.

"That's not what I'm hearing in your voice," he shot back.

"It wasn't him. It was the business. The hours. Being surrounded by hot little starlets who'd do anything if you'd sign them. Forever clawing your way up the charts. Keeping an eye on every move the competition makes—"

She choked on her words and gave him a guilty look, as if she shouldn't have let that slip. Her pretty mouth, the one he'd kissed so ardently, clamped tight. But the incriminating words had already left it, and Trent felt an eerie tingle crawl up his spine. It wasn't a pleasant feeling.

Isaiah. The music business. Clawing up the charts… signing starlets. It was all too much to be a coincidence. "Isaiah who?" he growled.

She shook her head stubbornly. Despite the warmth of the water, her skin felt clammy under his hands.

He tried again, insistently, hearing the blade-edge of displeasure in his own voice, but there was nothing he could do about it. "Isaiah who, Dakota?"

"I think…" She paused, then went on in anguish. "I think you already guessed."

He let her go abruptly and, unable to go backward because of the grotto wall behind him, stepped sideways. The skin-on-skin contact with her was too much to bear.

"Westfield," he guessed. The name alone was a bitter pill to chew on. Isaiah Westfield was the owner of Head-liners & Show-stoppers, the second largest privately owned talent and recording company in the country—after Trent's. He knew him well, and what he knew, he didn't like. Slippery as an eel, with an ambition as huge as the outdoors, and a will to achieve it that would stop at nothing. He lied with a pathological conviction and saw bribes as a legitimate business expense. He was a predator who relished the sexual power he held over the parade of marginally talented nineteen-year-olds who streamed out of the inner cities and small towns seeking a name in the music business.

Dakota had been involved in a relationship with *him?* "What were you thinking?" he couldn't stop himself from asking. "How'd you wind up with a son of a bitch like that?"

"It just happened," she said shortly, defensively. "He was smooth. He said all the right things. He took me places and showed me stuff. He introduced me to all the right people. I was a young writer, just starting out, and he made me feel smart and pretty—"

"You needed that punk to tell you you're beautiful?" he asked incredulously.

Dakota was already wading through the chest-high water, trying to find an exit point. Trying to get away from him. But the conversation wasn't over, not by a long shot. He followed her.

"What did he do to you? It can't be anything good, if you're so afraid of me you're falling over backward to get away, just because we're in the same business."

"Why do you care?"

"Why do I...?"

She was halfway up the ladder, her bare, shapely bottom just above his head, but she seemed oddly vulnerable in her nudity now, so he lowered his eyes.

"Why should you?" she repeated. "I'm nothing but a woman who slept with your enemy."

"I prefer the word 'competition,'" he responded dryly, although she wasn't far wrong. He loathed Westfield. There wasn't an honest bone in the man's body. He would stop at nothing to succeed, even if it meant infiltration and sabotage of the enemy camp. Westfield had been caught planting spies among Trent's staff in order to figure out his next business move. He was suspected of spreading scandalous rumors. He wasn't above feeding negative stories to the media.

For several seconds, Trent was sure his heart had

stopped beating, but when it kicked in again, it was racing so hard it almost choked him. "Westfield gave you that story," he guessed. He knew he'd hit the bull's-eye: dead-on and accurate. "He told you what to write about Shanique. It was a business ploy. You weren't after *her*. You were after *me*."

She was at the top of the pool, looking down at him. Dripping wet and naked, she reminded him of the painting over her big brass bed back at the cabin. The light of the moon made her face look pale, like cold ceramic. "I wasn't after anyone...."

"He used you to drag my name in the mud." He hauled himself out of the pool, just as naked as she, and towered over her. Anger made him light-headed. "Maybe I'm giving him too much credit. Maybe he didn't use you at all. You saw a chance to make a name for yourself, and you grabbed it."

She took her time retrieving her sodden dress from beside the pool, and began wringing water from it. Wordlessly, he thrust his dry shirt at her and dragged on his pants. She accepted it without acknowledgment and he watched as she threw it on. Then she stood half-turned, as if she couldn't bear to face him. He exhaled in rapid puffs, trying to regain control of his bitter rage. Trying and failing. He watched as she squeezed the water from her hair.

"I never set out to hurt you, or Shanique, or anyone," she said in a low voice. "I'm a journalist. I had a lead on a story—"

"You were sleeping with your source!"

"I slept with *you*," she snapped, "and the next morning you put me on to your own people. You *made* them speak to me, whether they wanted to or not."

"There's a difference," he argued.

"What difference?"

"I wanted to make you happy. I had no agenda, not like Westfield did. I was falling for you." He stopped, aware he'd said too much. Falling in love with Dakota. He'd known there was something there. It cried out to him every time he touched her and was always humming softly in his ears, kindling a low fire in his heart while he was making love to her. But he hadn't fully realized it until he'd said it. Falling for her. He would have laughed, if he wasn't so sickened. It was like falling out of a plane without a parachute.

The look on her face told him she'd heard his slip, and it was sinking in. Her mouth pursed, eyes scrunched, as if she wanted to cry from the pain. He felt instantly sorry…but was still too angry to back down. "I think I'm…" she started to say, but bit off her words. She began again. "I never slept with Isaiah for a story. He gave the leads to me, just like any man would give a gift to a woman. Just like you did…with this." She indicated the red-and-black bead necklace. "I had no idea that story would be so destructive. When it hit the press, Isaiah was gleeful. He practically broke out the champagne."

"He humiliated me and brought my entire business into disrepute. Why wouldn't he be thrilled?" He heard the ugliness in his voice, but couldn't extinguish it.

"That's when I recognized him for what he was. That's when I left him."

He let her revelation soak in for several seconds. "You left Westfield.…"

"Over you." She was wringing her hands, one choking the life out of the other. "And I'm sorry."

Hold her, a voice inside said. *She's admitted she has feelings for you, and you've done the same to her. Let bygones be bygones. Shake it off, and start over. You can have something with her, and you know it.* Instead, all he said was, "It's very late. We should go back to the cabin." And he began walking away.

Chapter 13

Dakota was never as grateful as she was the moment the lights of their cabin came into view. The prickle of grass under her bare feet was uncomfortable, water dripped down her back from her hair, and the light Caribbean breeze might as well have been a chilly Santa Amata blast against her damp skin, in spite of Trent's shirt.

Trent. Damn him. His reaction to finding out she'd been involved with his biggest rival was predictable, but unfair just the same. He could at least have given her a chance to explain herself…especially considering how intimate they'd been just moments before. But maybe that was asking too much. Sex was sex, and business was business. Men were really good at keeping the two separate.

He walked moodily beside her, as deep in his thoughts as she was in hers. He didn't seem to mind the cold that gnawed away at her bones. She didn't give in to the temptation to glance at him. Her heavy heart ached. Life was so strange; it could turn on a dime. One minute he was sucking the juice from her like she was a tropical fruit, and the next the distance between them had become a chasm—at the mere mention of her former lover.

Well, it was more than just Isaiah; she understood that. She'd meant it when she'd said that it had never been her intention to harm him or ruin Shanique's career. If anything, her story had served as the impetus for Shanique to get help…so everything had worked out, hadn't it? She'd honestly taken the story in good faith. But how to convince him of that? Would he ever give her the chance?

Would she *want* him to? Her anger rose to match his. It was stupid; she was mad because he was mad, offended because he'd taken offense. All she wanted to do was put a solid wall between them, dry off, get into bed and sulk in peace.

"Give me your hand."

"Huh?"

They were at the low porch steps, and Trent was already grasping her hand to help her up them. Without thinking, she snatched it away. "I'm not infirm," she stuttered as an excuse.

"No," he said softly, "but you *are* a lady." All the same, he didn't try to take her hand again. They stood at the door, and there was a clink as he began sorting through the keys in his pocket. He found the right one, but as he inserted it into the lock, it gave under his hand. He threw her a puzzled look. "Didn't you lock this?"

Damn. "No, I… I was just wandering around the

garden. I didn't mean to go far. Anke told me how safe it is here, how people in Tobago don't bother to lock up. I just pulled it shut...." She rummaged through the pocket of her soaking wet dress, to find it empty. She groaned. Her key was probably sitting at the bottom of the grotto. "I'm sorry."

He shook his head. "It's okay."

Still, male protective instincts being what they were, he pushed the door in and shepherded her behind him so she was shielded by his body as they entered. He was wearing nothing but his jeans, and she found herself pressed against his bare back, feeling the smooth, cool hardness of his muscle. She inched sideways, preparing to slip past him, impatient with his take-a-bullet-for-the-lady gesture, especially when there was no sign of danger.

As it turned out, he had the instincts of a jackal. With a bark in her direction, an order to get down, Trent hunched and sprang, crossing the cabin before she realized something was wrong. There was a crash of glass, and she heard him yell.

Someone was in their cabin.

Caring more for his safety than hers, she ran in after him, one hand outstretched, searching for a weapon and finding only a wine bottle. Deciding it would do in a pinch, she ran to the commotion in the center of the small living room. Fear and shock thumped in her veins.

Then a woman started screaming. Dakota felt for the lights, as puzzled as she was scared. Hadn't she left them on? The glare flooded the room, illuminating Trent and the person whose arms he'd pinned to her sides.

Shanique.

The diva was clutching a shot glass, and a bottle of premium Scotch whiskey sat on the coffee table. Dakota was sure it had come from the drink cabinet. The bottle was about one-third empty. Shanique was still wearing her stage clothes and makeup, even though the show had ended hours ago. Her elaborate hairdo was mussed, and she was cussing a blue streak. "Trent! What the hell! Let me go!"

He released her at once. His face was a mixture of surprise, anger and concern. "What're you doing here?" he asked.

"I heard there was an after-party at your place," she slurred. "How come I didn't get an invite?"

"There's no after-party, and you know it," he answered firmly, snatching the bottle away from the table. She grabbed for it, and a struggle ensued. She protested with a guttural snarl, but he held it high, out of her reach. "Enough, Shanique."

She cursed, and turned for comfort to the little that was left in her glass. It was only then that Shanique realized Dakota was standing there. Her black-eyed squint took in everything, from Dakota's dripping hair to the man's shirt draped around her, and her bare, damp legs. Her lips curled in a snarl. "Seems you really *did* have a party. Guess I wasn't invited because it's a skanks-only event."

No way was Dakota letting that go without retaliation. "If that were the case," she ground out, "you'd have been the guest of honor."

Shanique drained her glass and tossed it to the floor among the shards of a wine bottle, which had fallen over when Trent had run into the room. Her exquisite face was ugly with rage. "Oh, tell me you ain't looking for a piece of this!" She advanced on Dakota, holding her hands out, beckoning her like a street brawler.

Dakota didn't flinch. "The condition you're in, you're probably seeing double. You wouldn't know which one of me to hit."

Shanique lunged, and in reflex, Dakota brought her hands up before her face. She wasn't one for catfights, but she wasn't going to be a victim, either.

Trent stepped swiftly between them, grasping Shanique by the arms and forcing her into a chair. "Do not get up," he ordered.

"You ain't the boss of me," she whined. One of her false eyelashes had come askew, and she rubbed her eye vigorously. It started tearing up.

"I am, actually," he answered grimly. "So knock it off." He turned to Dakota. "Can you get that glass cleaned up?"

Her mouth fell open, but before she could suggest a destination slightly south of hell, he reasoned, "I don't want anybody to get cut."

As much as she wanted to, she couldn't argue with that, so she stomped off, rummaging around in the kitchen for a broom and dustpan.

"How'd you know where I was staying?" she heard Trent ask.

"I heard you talking to your secretary," Shanique replied. "It's not like you'd tell me," she added with a hoarse, bitter laugh. "And why should you? Holed up here with some no-talent piece of trash you picked up."

Before Dakota could protest, Trent cut her off. "Leave Dakota alone."

"But you're sleeping with her! Don't deny it!"

Trent didn't try.

Shanique went on, more agitated by the second. "How could you? She hates me. She hates you! All she's doing is pumping you for stories."

Dakota slipped silently between them and began sweeping up the shards of glass, wishing she could dump the razor-sharp contents of the dustpan on Shanique's messed-up head.

"Pumping…" Shanique repeated. Her laugh turned into a cough. "That what she did, Trent baby? That how she gets her stories?" She leaned toward Trent so the poison she was spitting could better find its target. "Did she pump them out of you or did she suck them out of you?"

Dakota gasped at the crudeness of the statement. She threw the broom to the floor. "Listen, sister…!"

Shanique changed direction fast, and played the pity card, slumping with her face in her hands and mewing. "I need another drink."

"No, you don't," Trent said. "You had enough."

"Please, please," she wheedled. She got up, spine curved, crocodile tears ruining her smeared makeup, and walked over to Trent. "Oh, baby, help me. Just one more, and I'll be good. I promise."

He shook his head. "You promised a lot of things. You promised you'd stay clean."

"I tried, but I can't do it without you."

Trent resisted, gently but firmly. "I'm there for you. I've always been there for you. If you want me to get you back into rehab, I will."

"That's not what I meant, and you know it." Shanique pouted like a six-year-old.

Dakota watched as Shanique wrapped her arms around him, a woman almost six feet tall curling up against his chest like a child. "Don't," he said, but didn't push her away.

Dakota felt a pilot light of jealousy ignite inside her. She set down the dustpan. She shouldn't have to stand here and watch a woman she didn't like, a woman who hated her, press her demonically curvaceous body against the man she loved.

The man she loved. She choked, not sure if that revelation upset her more than the sight before her. Trent heard the sound, cut off in her throat, and looked at her over Shanique's head. She wasn't sure what he could read, but she was desperately hoping it wasn't the truth.

Something arced between them, and his brows lifted. In a moment of pure clarity, those toffee eyes took in everything. It was like being held in a spotlight beam, imprisoned and unable to look away, and then being sliced open, laid bare.

He *knew she loved him.* He knew how she felt, just at a time when they were in the middle of their worst argument ever. Just when he was all but bleeding from what he saw as her betrayal. She looked away, unable to bear his piercing gaze.

There was a furious shriek of protest and a streak of obscenities as Trent disentangled himself from Shanique's grasp. "How dare you do this to me?" she squawked. "You love me!"

Dakota searched for Trent's eyes again, but couldn't catch them. Either he was studiously avoiding her gaze, or he was so focused on Shanique that he was barely aware that she was there. His face was both somber and sad. "I used to."

The woman refused to accept the death knell of their soured relationship. "Even after I broke up with you,

you loved me. Even when I was in rehab, after I got clean again, you loved me, and you know it. You begged for a chance."

The look that crossed Trent's face then was so gentle and nostalgic it was almost unbearable. "I did."

Shanique stamped her high-heeled foot in frustration, arms out before her, demanding an explanation. "So, what happened?" She answered her question herself. Her eyes, full of hellfire, swung toward Dakota, one arm rising accusingly in her direction, diamond-tipped finger glinting like a tiny blade. "It's because of *her!*"

"No," Trent said softly, as if it pained him to say it. "It's because of you."

This was too much. Dakota shouldn't be part of this intensely private conversation. She stumbled from the room. "Excuse me. I'll…leave you to it."

It was as if she'd never been there. As she hastened for the sanctuary of her bedroom, voices floated after her, Shanique's shrill and angry, and Trent's placating but implacable.

Dakota shut the door, leaning against it as if the Hound of the Baskervilles was clawing at the other side. Panting like a long-distance runner, she stripped Trent's shirt off. It smelled too good. It made him feel too close. She grabbed a towel, scrubbed at her body, then dragged on a T-shirt and jeans. Her hair clung to her face in tangles; she shoved it out of the way.

She'd gone and done the dumbest thing she could possibly do—fall in love with Trent Walker. What had it taken, three, four days? Seemed there was no minimum time allowed for stupidity. Another powerful music business man, another creative, ambitious, driven creature, sunk chest-deep in the industry that both scared and fascinated her.

What was it about such men that attracted her so much? Was it that they were a part of the music business she loved? Or maybe it was time she started separating the two men in her mind. When she was with Isaiah, she'd been younger and greener, impressed by his power and flash. With Isaiah, what you saw was what you got. Under Trent's tough-guy shell, he was different. She'd seen the real him many times since they'd landed in Tobago. He was one of the good guys. He was worthy of love.

She clapped her hands to her face in incredulity. Love. Trent. No.

It's not so bad, a little voice whispered in her ear. *He's not Isaiah. He's a different man. A better man.* Trent was smart and sexy. The *wabine* in the jar on her dresser brought to mind the group of little children he'd fed. He was kind to kids. He'd been kind to *her,* a woman he'd disliked and didn't trust, when she'd needed a place to sleep.

Would loving Trent Walker be so bad?

Outside, the volume of the argument rose; Shanique was screaming, an incoherent river of sound. It was interspersed by a low rumble: Trent applying reason where she had none. Here Dakota was, alone, her body still sore from an intense sexual encounter with a man she just discovered she loved, while he was just outside, trying to talk his drunk, hysterical ex-lover down from the ledge. It was the stuff of daytime talk shows.

Even as Dakota tried not to listen, the ruckus outside subsided. The quiet was almost more ominous. A knock at her door scared her out of her skin. She leaped around to face it. "Yes?"

"Dakota." Trent's voice, deep and sober.

She opened up. He was wearing a clean shirt and had put his shoes on. Not a good sign. He looked troubled and weary. "She's in pretty bad shape," he began, but stopped himself with an ironic grunt at his own understatement. "I'm taking her back to her yacht."

The jealousy lifted its head inside her, a serpent that needed to be wrestled into submission. Would Shanique have to be held again, like the last time? *Comforted?*

"I called her manager," he told her, as if he could smell her irrational fear. "He'll be waiting by the time we get there. I'll hand her over and make sure she's safe." His eyes snared hers. "I'm coming straight back. Then… We'll talk."

"Talk…about what?" she hedged. She wasn't ready for the honesty he'd demand of her. She needed some time.…

His mouth twitched in what could almost have been a smile. "Don't be foolish. There's a lot to say."

"It's two in the morning!" she blurted.

Now he really did smile. "Okay. So we'll sleep, and first thing in the morning, we'll talk." He brushed away a floppy lock of her hair. "Okay?"

She nodded, too overwhelmed to speak.

"It's late. Streets are clear. I won't be an hour." He paused, waiting for her to answer, and then frowned. He tilted his head, as if listening for something, turned abruptly, and hurried back to the silent living room. Dakota also realized it was way too silent. She followed him, taut with dread.

A grated obscenity from Trent confirmed her fears. Shanique wasn't there.

"She took my car keys," he groaned. Of one accord, they looked at the coffee table, where the bottle of whiskey stood. What was left in it rippled gently, as if someone had slammed it down after taking a hearty swig.

Side by side, moving like a single, fluid animal, Dakota and Trent bolted from the cabin, up the path, in the direction of the parking lot.

Chapter 14

The parking lot was bathed in an eerie, orange light. Mosquitoes, moths and other bugs swirled under the overhead lamps, dancing like angels in sunbeams. The night air should have been silent at this hour, but wasn't. The cries of frogs and owls sliced into the silence, interspersed with the shrieks of bats. Cutting across their late-night serenade was the low purr of Trent's rented BMW.

The windows were down, and Dakota could see Shanique, her long fingers wrapped around the steering wheel in a death grip.

"Stop!" Trent shouted.

In answer to his warning cry, she turned her head, and as she did so, her cheeks glistened with moisture. Distraught, she turned away. The engine roared, deep and guttural, a dinosaur awakened from slumber, and the car jerked forward, tires screaming.

Trent was no longer at Dakota's side. He loped across
the lot, darting between parked cars into the open. The
lights on the Beemer turned him into a lone performer
on a huge stage. The car lurched in his direction, and
he darted sideways, coming at the driver's side from
an angle.

For Dakota, thought and emotion were one. Panic
and dread. *He's going to get himself killed.* She wanted
to shout a warning, but couldn't.

"Stop," Trent bellowed again. "Shanique, hold up!"

The tires screeched in defiance.

Dakota realized she was praying as she caught a
glimpse of Shanique's ghastly face, weirdly silver, and
a pair of hollow eyes.

As Shanique jerked toward the exit, Trent tried again,
grasping at the driver's door, and Dakota wondered if
he was insane enough to try to reach in and grab the
wheel. The car swerved, like a big dog trying to shake
a smaller one off its back, and Trent was thrown clear,
backward into a dense patch of deep red ginger lilies.
With a whimper of pure fear, Dakota ran to him.

He was already getting to his feet, brushing away
her frantic hands and turning in the direction of the car.
It knifed into a spin, and skated off the drive, gravel
spraying under its wheels. The car slid sideways and
crashed into the large, arched wrought-iron Rapture
sign at the entrance, finally coming to a stop there. The
sign groaned at the insult, and the post that had taken
the brunt of the impact slowly listed to one side.

Dakota was there just seconds behind Trent. There
was a gouge along the entire passenger side of the
Beemer, as if a huge hand had tried to peel it open
like a tin banana. Trent yanked on the driver's door,

and mercifully, it was unlocked. Shanique was buried in a white, marshmallowy airbag cloud. The pungent, chemical smell of the airbag burned Dakota's nostrils.

Trent asked urgently. "Shanique, are you okay?" He pressed down on the now deflating airbag, trying to see her face.

There was an answering groan, and a curse. The un-ladylike epithet filled Dakota with relief. It meant she was conscious, at least.

A solid presence at her back made her gasp, and she spun around to see a dense black shadow hovering over them. Her panic was quelled by a familiar baritone.

"It's Declan. What happened?"

The resort owner's thick locks were held back with a rubber band, and it didn't take Dakota more than a few seconds to notice he was wearing nothing but a very brief pair of shorts. The stark white of the fabric threw into contrast the utter blackness and perfection of his skin. Chiding herself for her momentary distraction, she stepped aside and let him through. He was, after all, a doctor.

Her arms folded against the chilly ocean breeze, she watched as Declan looked Shanique over thoroughly, not even allowing her to exit the car until he was satisfied that she hadn't been seriously hurt. As Shanique struggled to fight him off, he methodically and purposefully ran his hands down her limbs, peered into her eyes, and examined her head for blood or bruising. Even Trent, the take-charge go-getter, didn't intervene, bowing to a more knowledgeable authority.

After several minutes, Declan held out both arms, easing Shanique out of the smashed vehicle and settling her on the grass. "She doesn't seem to be injured," he murmured. "But we're still going to have her checked out."

Trent was already on the phone with Enrique and nodded. He paused the conversation, asking, "Should we call an ambulance?"

Declan's beautifully sculpted lips curved in a wry smile. "This is a small island. The time it would take to rustle one up, you could already have driven her to the hospital."

Trent threw a rueful glance at his wrecked rental. "Don't think I'll be driving that soon." After a few more quick words into the phone, he dropped to his knees. Gently cupping Shanique's chin, turning her face to his so she could focus on what he was saying, he spoke, enunciating carefully in case she was too deep in shock to understand. "Enrique's on his way. He'll be here in a few minutes, and then he'll take you to the hospital."

"Don't need a hosp—" Shanique began, then tore herself away, rolled over, and threw up in the grass.

For the next several minutes, Dakota stood on the sidelines, feeling useless. Declan popped back into his cabin, the closest one to the entrance, and returned fully dressed, bearing a blanket, which he placed around Shanique's shoulders. He cleaned her face with wet washcloths, and kept her alert until Enrique's headlights cut across them. He slid to a stop, barely avoiding the leaning iron sign, yanked up his emergency brake and left the engine running as he leaped out with surprising agility for a man of his size.

The obese man huffed and puffed over, his sweaty face a picture of worry. "How is she?" he gasped like an asthmatic. Even in his anxiety, he still took the time to spear Dakota with a hostile look.

"Fine, I think," Declan answered before Trent could. "But I'd recommend some X-rays. I've already called ahead to the hospital. They're expecting her." Quickly, he gave directions, and between them, they settled Shanique into the back seat of Enrique's car.

By the time Trent turned to Dakota, she already knew the decision he'd made.

"I need to go with her. Make sure she really is all right."

"It's okay," she murmured, and it actually was.

He prepared to get in with Enrique, but with a fluid, underarm motion, Declan tossed something silver and jangly at him. He caught it in midarc and frowned down into his hand. Dakota leaned forward to see what it was, too. Trent pressed a button, and a nearby SUV beeped and turned on its headlights.

"That one's mine," Declan explained. "I'll ride with the lady, so I can keep an eye on her on the way down. Dakota can ride with you."

Dakota's surprise must have shown on her face, because he gave her an encouraging smile. She felt suddenly transparent, as if it was obvious to Declan how she felt about Trent, in spite of her insistence about them just being colleagues. There was something alive and intense between them, something undeniable, and the man could tell. He was, after all, an expert in love, sex, and relationships. Embarrassed, she wondered if she gave off some sort of glow.

"I know you don't want her to be stuck in the cabin all on her lonesome," Declan added. "And I'm sure Dakota would rather be with you." And then the devil actually winked.

* * *

The sun was already up by the time Dakota, Trent and Declan made it back to Rapture. But it did little good, as one of those sudden Caribbean downpours overtook them and the brilliant blue sky that had made them feel so welcome all week was a dismal gray. Water trickled down bushes and dripped from the samaan tree outside their cabin. The grass around it was littered with battered red blossoms. Birds gleefully chattered in the branches with their tail feathers spread. White egrets stomped around on the ground, nabbing hapless worms that had wriggled from their burrows in an effort to save themselves from drowning.

They said goodbye to Declan at the entrance and headed for their cabin. Beside her, Trent was deep in thought. He looked as bone-weary as she felt. Her heart went out to him. She wondered if he'd consent to sharing her bed this morning, not to make love but to sleep in each other's arms.

"This is bad," he said.

"She didn't break any bones, at least. No concussion, no internal damage…"

He shook his head as if that was inconsequential. "Shanique's damage isn't visible to the naked eye. Her problems can't be fixed with a bandage or a cast."

He was right. Whatever therapy she'd had, it hadn't worked. Trent's diva would need long-term, professional help.

"Do you think she'll be able to perform tonight?"

He gave her a look that said what she was suggesting was madness. "She insists she can, but I won't let her. She's too fragile."

"But she's the feature act!"

He acknowledged her point. "I know. I've already called my people. They're going to have another performer on the island by this afternoon. It'll be someone big enough to keep the audience happy. Her publicist will have to come up with a reasonable excuse for her pulling out."

She thought about Shanique's exquisite performance last night and how it had moved her to tears. What a terrible loss to the festival and its audience, if they couldn't experience what she had. "Are you sure? She was sober and coherent when we left her."

"She can perform, but I'm worried about what would come after. You saw what happened last night. She almost lost it. She could crack at any time, and if it happens onstage… Well, her reputation is on the edge as it is. A story about that could tip it over. And the festival is crawling with journalists.…" A thought crossed his face, like a time-lapse video of a creek drying. He didn't need to voice it.

Dakota looked away. Only one journalist knew exactly what had happened *after* the concert, because only one had been there to witness the drama. It was the kind of story that would make the front page of every entertainment section, take top billing on any news blog.… And only she could truly tell it.

The idea made her sick.

They reached the cabin without exchanging another word, but Dakota could hear Trent's thoughts churning. He followed her in, kicking the door shut, and stripped off his rain-soaked shirt right there at the entrance. As tired and disturbed as she was by the thick tension between them, his lithe, fit body caught her attention. She wondered if he was going to reach for her, but chided herself for her silliness as he blundered to his room to find dry clothes.

"You should change," came his disembodied voice.

How do you want me to change? her stress-muddled mind asked, and then she understood he was referring to her wet clothing. She did as he suggested. As she toweled off her hair for the second time in six hours, she spotted her phone, forgotten in last night's insanity, lying on the dressing table next to the *wabine* in its jar. The red light at the tip flashed a frantic signal. She checked it: 6 missed calls, all from the same number. Her editor's.

Double dammit. She'd spent so much time moping yesterday she hadn't written a word. She was contracted to submit two stories twice a week, and in a rare slipup, she'd neglected to complete her assignment. There'd be a gaping hole in her column tomorrow, and her editor was probably mad enough to bite the head off a bat.

She desperately wanted to sleep, but knew she wouldn't be able to rest until she returned the call and ate a big slice of humble pie. The phone was answered on the third ring. "Where the hell have you been?" the woman on the other end snapped.

"I'm sorry, Maryse," she began, "I know I was unprofessional—"

"You're damn right it was unprofessional. You'd better have a good excuse."

Dakota almost laughed at the idea of explaining her lapse: *you see, I've gone and fallen in love with this man, and I can't get him out of my head long enough to write a sentence....* Instead, she said, "A couple of things happened..."

"They better be things you can write about. Your papers are clamoring for copy."

She thought about the copy she could have given them, if she wanted to. A singing star going on a bender the night of her return to the stage…a huge talent crashing, literally and figuratively. She could already see the headlines.

Maryse cut through her thoughts. "You went to the concert, at least." Her tone made it clear that not doing that much should be a capital offense. After Dakota confirmed, Maryse seemed a little mollified, "Well, how was it? How was Shanique's comeback?"

"She was…magnificent." *And then, she blew it,* Dakota could have said. Should have said. She took the phone away from her ear for a second and cradled it against her breast. Why wasn't she saying more? She'd messed up bad enough by being late with her column, but withholding a story from her editor was treason. Then she remembered that ghastly face, streaked with tears under the parking-lot lights, and compassion made her decision for her. Shanique didn't deserve to be exposed in her darkest moment. Nobody did.

She brought the phone to her ear again. Maryse was barking instructions for her to send her stories off before nightfall, especially one about Shanique's return to the stage. That, she could handle. "No problem, Maryse," she promised. "You'll get your Shanique story. Before the day's over." The line went dead.

Dakota set the phone down, sighing in the realization that there would be no sleep for her this morning. She'd have to start right away if… She turned to see Trent standing in the doorway. His face was as dark as the clouds outside.

"Couldn't wait, huh?" His voice ground like metal on metal.

"What?" she gasped.

"Maryse Maitlin is your editor, isn't she? Tell me it's a coincidence that you were on the phone with her ten minutes after you get back from seeing Shanique in a hospital." His jaw was tightly clenched. "Already shopping around your next career-defining story?"

The insinuation hit her square in the solar plexus. "I was returning her call!"

He curled his lip in disbelief. "And promising her a story on Shanique."

She waved her arms in protest against the unfair allegation. "On her *performance!*"

"And not a word on what happened after?" He looked at her with disgust. "You expect me to believe that?"

"Yes, I do!"

He didn't seem to have heard her. "A story like that would set her back as bad as her addiction. She needs something to shoot for, and music is all she has. But I don't expect a predator like you—"

Her outrage matched his. "I watched a woman almost kill herself last night, and you believe all I'm after is a story? That is what you think of me?"

He stopped, for one minute, unsure of himself.

She thundered on. "You kissed me. You made love to me. But when the chips are down, you instantly revert to the old opinion you've always had of me. A scavenger. A predator."

"I walk in and you're phoning in a hot story—"

"My conversation with my editor is my own damn business," she snapped. "I don't need to justify myself to you. What bothers me is that you're prepared to think the worst of me the second any doubt arises. Bad enough you think I let Isaiah manipulate me into trying to ruin you—"

He let out a harsh groan of frustration. "He's the last person I want to talk about right now—"

Too upset to care that she was goading a bull, she rushed on. "Oh, *I* have to tolerate the sight of your ex draping herself all over you, but you can't stand it when I mention Isaiah?"

"You're jealous!" he asserted, as if that explained away her ire.

Like hell. Jealousy was for the weak. She was *mad.* "Don't be stupid. I'm just tired of tiptoeing around that woman and all her hang-ups. And I hate that you hold your cards tighter than a poker player whenever the subject comes up."

The mottling under his skin told her his temper was well ablaze. "Maybe I'm afraid if you spotted my ace, you'd broadcast it to everyone at the table."

She flinched under the attack on her character and tried to drag the conversation back to its core. "Trent," she said patiently, "you've been in show business long enough to know nothing stays a secret for long. This is the digital age, and just because we're on a tiny island doesn't mean what happened here, or some version of what happened here, won't get out."

"I know that—" he grated.

She cut across him. "A hospital is a public place, and Shanique's face is well known. It's only a matter of time before an orderly with a cell phone camera—"

"Don't you think I haven't thought of that? I have PR people headed over there to do as much damage control as they can...."

"Then why are you so worried about me writing something?"

He leaned closer, the honey color of his eyes replaced by a frightening, deep darkness. "Because I *know* I can't trust the orderlies. I *know* I can't trust whatever opportunistic reporter is willing to jump on her story and take it for all he can get. But you…" His pause was final, condemning. "You, I was beginning to trust. I was beginning to…" He chewed off what he was about to say.

Love me? wondered Dakota in anguish.

"I'm not afraid of a story. I'm a big boy, and I've handled worse. What would really burn is where the story came from. *Who* it came from."

"And what burns *me*," she countered, "is that nothing I say would convince you that I wouldn't do such a thing." She crossed her arms in frustration. "Next you'll be accusing me of writing a tell-all about what the great Trent Walker's like in bed!"

He shook his head vehemently. "Not even you would—" He recognized the cruelty of his words and tried to bite them off, but it was too late. "I'm sorry," he began, then stalled.

She sank onto the bed, exhausted, and let her face fall into her hands. His theory that their day and night personas could exist separate from each other was fundamentally flawed. They could make wild and wonderful love all night, but when they rolled out of bed in the morning she would still be Dakota the writer and he'd still be Trent the producer.

The idea that they were in love was an illusion. A magician's trick, and Declan had been the one waving the magic wand. Rapture was a warm cocoon in which sexual desire and heated emotions thrived, but sooner or later, they both had to crawl back out to reality. And that reality was simple and brutal: she and Trent weren't meant for each other. Their compatibility existed solely on a sexual plane; in everything else, there might as well be a force field around each of them that the other couldn't breach.

"I don't..." she began, and then stopped. "I don't believe in magic."

When she glanced up at him, he had cocked his head to one side, like a curious animal. "What?"

"This isn't real, Trent. It never was."

The realization of what she was saying dawned slowly on his face. She could tell he knew what was coming, and was already forming an argument against it. "I don't believe in magic, either. I believe in compatibility—"

She shot up off the bed, desperate to resist his persuasive powers, afraid she would give in. "You call this compatibility? We can't go two days without jumping down each other's throats!"

"We're compatible in bed," he countered.

"Sex isn't love."

He left his position in her doorway and stepped closer. She prayed he wouldn't touch her, but he did. His hand was warm on her shoulder. "It's a place to start," he said.

Stop touching me, she pleaded wordlessly. *You're making me weak.* She resisted his pull with everything she had. "It's not enough."

"That's because you haven't given us enough time. It's only been a few days—"

She had to break their contact. She almost fell over backward trying. "Us? What us?"

Pain at her retreat was etched around his taut mouth. "I see two people who're having teething problems, the kind you get at the start of any new relationship."

She didn't want to listen, because if she did, she might believe. "And I see two people who have nothing but suspicion and bitter memories to build on, and that, my friend, is like building a castle on wet sand."

He was silent for a very long time…too long. He folded his arms across his chest, as if he was trying to keep his heart in. "What do you want me to do, then?" he asked eventually. "How can I fix this?"

Nice offer…except it couldn't be fixed. She knew that what she would say next couldn't be unsaid. "I want you to leave me be. I'm going home."

He shook his head. "You can't mean that."

She looked away, unable to keep her eyes on his face. "Please, Trent, go to your room. I have to pack." Leaving before the festival was over would throw her column into shambles, and she'd catch hell for that, but it was better than…this.

He hesitated, half turned, and then faced her again. "I'd figured you for a lot of things, most of them not good. This week, you changed my mind. But I never figured you for a quitter." With a heavy sigh, he walked out of her room, shutting the door behind him.

She found the strength not to cry, shoving the tears into the background by focusing on what she needed to do. She called the lobby and requested one of the resort taxis, and was advised it would be ready in ten minutes. She dragged her suitcase out, remembering how Trent had rummaged through it in the chaos of the power outage to find her some clothes. It almost made her smile. That was the night of the iguana, when he'd first kissed her under the samaan tree, while the blue-and-white charms tinkled like wind chimes.

Illusion. Declan's smoke and mirrors. What she felt for Trent was an illusion, and the sooner she got away from Rapture and its heady influence, the better she would feel. She glanced about her room. Her *wabine* was still swimming in its bottle, calm and serene. Trent would feed it for her, so she wasn't worried. She snapped the suitcase shut, strapped her carry-on to it, and headed for the door.

Something stopped her, a nagging sensation that she'd forgotten something. But what? There was nothing under the bed, nothing in the bathroom. Unconsciously, responding to unnatural warmth, she put her hands to her throat, and encountered the circle of hard, red beans. Her jumbie bead necklace, the "binding charm" as Declan insisted, that Trent had given her.

She sucked her teeth, struggling with the clasp in an effort to remove it. She was about to tear it from around her neck when the clasp gave way. She held it coiled in the palm of her hand. A hundred black eyes stared back at her from their red sockets. Accusing. She shuddered and dropped it next to the fish as if it was hot. That was one bit of magic she wasn't taking with her. The speckled, spiral-shell pendant lay in the middle, her wish unwished.

When she stepped into the hallway between the two rooms, Trent's door was closed. Walking past it, dragging her bags, took as much effort as a spaceship tearing itself away from the gravitational pull of the earth. She'd escaped without being burned too badly. She counted herself lucky for that.

Chapter 15

If Trent looked any sexier, the cops were liable to arrest him for disturbing the peace. He glowed in the summer sunshine. As he walked onto the bandstand at the center of De Menzes Park in downtown Santa Amata, the crowd of music lovers—mainly young women—completely lost it. They cheered, whistled, and screamed, as if he was one of the music stars he represented, rather than the man behind it all.

Dakota hugged herself as she watched the action unfold on the wide-screen TV in her office. Over the past three months, she'd seen pictures of him in the paper, or glimpsed him as she clicked through the channels, but she always turned the page or kept on clicking. This afternoon, for some reason, she couldn't look away.

The man bided his time until the cheers died down and then stepped up to the mike. "Thank you," he boomed. His audience, including Dakota, waited for what he was to say next—but she was more enthralled by the sound of his voice than what he had to say. "Outlandish Music is delighted to announce that we have signed a five-year contract with the Anderson triplets. Their first album will be released this fall." The teeny-boppers in the audience whooped.

Dakota had to admit he'd pulled off quite a coup. He'd just won a bidding war between some of the best studios—including Isaiah Westfield's—to produce the country's most promising boy band. Identical 20-year-old triplets, tall, reedy white boys who looked like they were bred on an Idaho farm but who sounded like a cross between Nat King Cole and Common. The pundits were guaranteeing this trio would be the next big chart-buster.

She was glad for him. Honestly. She just wasn't so sure if she was ready to stand there and watch him on TV. He seemed so self-assured, and so alive, it was almost as if he was consciously projecting a part of himself through the airwaves, directly at her. Honeyed eyes held the camera, pierced it.

But that was stupid. That was her heart talking—if it could talk at all, considering it was clenching so tight it was a wonder blood was getting pumped around her body. God, she missed him. How could you miss someone you'd only known a few days, she wondered. She answered her own question: *same way you could fall in love with one.*

A sound behind made her jump. Kiara Caruthers walked in, her arms loaded with books. "Where you want these?" she puffed.

Dakota patted her cheek self-consciously, wondering if her new assistant could tell she was flushing. While

Dakota hadn't fired her previous one for botching her hotel booking in Tobago, she'd had to let her go once her own fortunes had declined. Kiara came with her new position as editor of a music magazine, and though Dakota had only met her twice, she was sure they'd get along great. The young woman was enthusiastic about her job. Hell, she was enthusiastic about everything.

Dakota wrenched her eyes away from the image on the screen, and her thoughts of what might have been. Of what she'd messed up through cowardice and anger. It was better not to think about it, not to dwell too long on the aching loneliness she couldn't escape, and the bitter regret that kept her up at night. She needed to teach herself to forget.

Moreover, she needed to remind herself why she'd left him in the first place. Love needed to be based on trust, not good sex. If they couldn't have that, they had nothing. The regrets she nursed at night were always washed away in the daylight by the hope that she'd done the right thing. Their affair was over, and it would stay that way.

She glanced around at the empty shelves in her spacious new office. "Over there, I guess," she said, pointing at a walnut bookcase that had little on it but a Lucite award for journalism and a framed photo of herself and her parents.

But Kiara had dumped the box of books at her feet and was staring at the screen, one hand on her hip. She gave a dramatic groan. "Oh, man, he looks good today." Then she laughed. "What am I saying? He looks good every day." She gave Dakota a broad grin, unaware of the irrational flare of jealousy she'd lit inside her.

"I'm sure Walker will get those boys straight to the

top of the charts, and keep 'em there," Kiara continued. "At least it'll keep him busy until Shanique comes
up for air."

Dakota winced at the mention of the name. The blogs
and media houses were abuzz with speculation about
Shanique's whereabouts. It was a slam dunk to assume
she was holed up in an expensive rehab center somewhere, but fans had variously reported spotting her in
the U.S., Switzerland, the Caymans and even Australia.

But regardless of where she was hiding, everyone
knew she was in therapy for drug and alcohol abuse.
Despite the strenuous efforts of Shanique's publicist
and Trent's damage-control experts, the story of her
car wreck and hospitalization became public knowledge in under 24 hours. Every entertainment writer,
every music newshound, had been all over it. Everyone
except for Dakota. And the consequences had sent her
career spinning off its axis.

She looked down at the box at Kiara's feet. Glad for
an excuse not to stare at Trent's image any longer, she
lifted it with a grunt and began stacking the books herself. She'd only begun moving in this morning, but it
wasn't as if she had a whole lot of stuff to bring over
from her home office; she'd always been a minimalist.

It was good to be working again. Her silence on the
Shanique story had not gone down well with her syn-
dicate, and her lame excuses about fleeing Tobago in
midfestival for "personal reasons" had been met with
steely disapproval. They dumped her, and her column
disappeared from dozens of newspapers across the
country. The blow to her reputation, and her income,
had been severe.

Then the job of editing a steadily growing music

magazine had turned up. The salary was excellent, and the work challenging. It would be interesting being on the other side of the entertainment news, editing rather than writing, but she still got to use her nose for news. Even more than before, as half her time would be spent looking out for good stories and assigning them to the writers she thought were best for them. What was more, working in a new environment, carving out a new niche for herself, would keep her very busy. Way too busy to spend much time thinking about Tobago, Rapture or Trent.

The press conference on TV wrapped up, or at least Trent's part of it. The blond triplets had taken the stage after him and were belting out their new single with carefully choreographed moves, to the appreciative screams of the young audience.

Kiara snapped out of her Trent-induced stupor and slapped her forehead. "Oh, damn, Dakota, I almost forgot."

"What?" she answered idly, wiping the dustcover of an old book before shelving it.

"You got the weirdest package just now. Hand-delivered, by courier."

Dakota lifted her head, frowning. A package delivered to her office, on the first day of the job? "Are you sure it's for me, or the previous editor?" That had to be it. Few people in the industry even knew she was here yet. It wasn't possible that the package could be meant for her specifically.

"Got your name on it," Kiara yelled as she popped through the door. She returned, holding the item gingerly. "And guess what: it's alive!"

This, she had to see. Dakota followed Kiara to her

desk and watched as the young woman set the package gingerly down. It was a large foam crate, open at the top. She peered in, alert, curious, almost excited.

And froze.

Spotting her hesitation, Kiara offered, "Want me to take it out for you?"

Dakota was pretty sure she nodded, because Kiara carefully withdrew a glass fishbowl, fully equipped with all the pumps and filters the creatures needed to stay alive. A glass lid was held in place by a strip of tape. Swimming just above the blue gravel, looking none too pleased at being moved, was a pair of brilliantly colored red and blue tropical fish. They were long and slender, with gossamer fins like a butterfly's.

"Didn't know you liked tropical fish," Kiara chirped, oblivious to Dakota's shock. She rummaged around in the box again.

"Never had any," Dakota began, and then caught herself. "Well, I did once, but for a really short time."

"There's an envelope," Kiara said, and pulled out a pale green, rectangular object. "It just says 'Dakota.'"

Dakota didn't need to look at the writing to know who it was from. She was stunned, perplexed and apprehensive.

When Dakota didn't say anything—how could she?—Kiara asked, "Shall I open it?"

"No!" Dakota said hastily, almost snatching in from the girl's hand. "I…" For several seconds she was lost in the crisp black writing. Just her name, nothing else, and yet at the sight of that one scribble, her knees were failing to do their job. A letter from Trent, after three months' silence. Why?

Kiara looked vaguely chastened, as if she wasn't sure

what she'd done wrong, so Dakota said, partly by way of apology, but mostly because this letter could only be opened in private, "You can go on home now, Kiara."

Kiara's brows lifted in surprise. "Are you sure? It's only four-thirty...." She threw a glance at the fishbowl, and then at the letter, as if nothing waiting for her at home could be half as interesting.

Dakota nodded, surer than she'd ever been. "It's okay. We can finish unpacking tomorrow. We got a lot done today so you can...er..."

"Get lost," Kiara finished, with an understanding smile. "Thanks, boss." She headed for her office, where Dakota heard her getting her things together.

"See you in the morning," Dakota said distractedly. She ran her fingers along the seal. The envelope was bulky, strangely so, as if there was something odd-shaped inside.

She heard the door creak open, and then Kiara's voice floated toward her just before she walked through it. "There's fish food in the box, too. Your friend covers all his bases, huh?"

"Sure does," Dakota answered wryly, but refused to let Kiara bait her for any more information. She waited until the curious young woman gave up and left the office, shutting the door behind her.

Dakota leaned heavily against her desk, weighing the damn envelope like a psychic trying to guess at its contents. It was almost as if opening the letter would be tantamount to admitting to herself that she welcomed his gesture. But she didn't. If just seeing her name in his writing cut her raw, what would reading his note do to her?

Be strong, she chastised herself. This changed nothing. She slit the top with a fingernail, and shook the contents over the table. A coiled, red snake slithered out, causing her to jump, until she realized it wasn't a snake at all, but a string of beads. Its unblinking black eyes held hers. In the middle, the twisted shell swayed. The wishing shell.

Rubbish, she told herself, but the beads were as warm to her touch as if they'd been around her neck all along. The card, made of heavy, quality stock, didn't say much, but what it did say made her feel as though her thoughts were submerged in the bowl on the table, right beside those pretty little fish.

Congratulations on the new job.

That was it? After three months without a word, email or text, a bowl full of fish lands on her table? But what did she expect? The man was just being courteous. This wasn't an overture from an ex-lover; it was a gesture from one member of the music business to another. It meant nothing. She tore the card in two, and dropped it into the wastepaper basket where it belonged.

But try as she could, couldn't do the same to the necklace, her only souvenir of the time they'd spent together. She ran her thumb along the beads, one by one, as if she were praying in church. What if there was more to his message? The card said one thing, but the beads said something else. He could have left them behind at Rapture, for the chambermaid to throw out. But he'd brought them back with him, and now sent them to her.

He remembered. And it still meant something to him.

She slumped behind her desk, and let her forehead fall onto its cool surface. She was imagining things. Reading things that weren't there. The magic of Rapture was seducing her again. But oh, how badly she wanted to be seduced! She turned to the TV screen. The segment with Trent was long over, and they'd moved on to something else, but the image of his face was burned into her memory, just as his kisses were burned into her skin.

For the hundredth time, the thousandth time, she cursed herself for her hasty, foolish exit. Running away from the one good thing life was offering her, even as he begged her to give their love a chance. If only she could go back to that moment. No, not go back, go forward. If only she could have one more chance.

She realized she was clenching her fist so tightly it hurt. Slowly, she opened her hand. Her wishing shell had imprinted itself on the palm of her hand.

Chapter 16

She was certifiably insane, Dakota chided herself later that evening, as her GPS directed her to turn into a broad driveway at the end of the street, guided by the return address on the fishbowl's shipping label. As she entered the property, the subtle scent of summer flowers came to her, faint as a memory. It was like a ghost compared to the riotous smells of Tobago: sea salt, drying coral that burned the nose and flowers so perfumed it was almost a haze of fragrance.

Since she'd been back, every smell had been too vague, every color too weak, every note of music half-hearted. It was as if Tobago had ignited her senses, and returning home reduced them to the flicker of a dying candle. She sighed. *I'm a washed-out watercolor of myself. I left all my bright energy back on a tiny island.*

She took in her surroundings, as curious as she was anxious. Her only image of Trent at "home" was in a wooden cabin with white trimming that looked like sugar frosting. This was where he *really* lived. The garden could have been kept as harshly maintained as the others on the street, with clipped hedges and flower beds lined by a ruler. Instead, wild summer flowers grew everywhere, as if a child had thrown handfuls of mixed seeds into the air like confetti.

She'd expected the house to be large; she hadn't expected it to be so tastefully understated. It was a symphony of muted hues, and its generous use of timber and stone made it almost seem rustic. This was where one of the most powerful men in music chose to live? Where was the glamour, the ostentation?

This house reflected the Trent she'd known, not his public persona of power, wealth and control, but the easy, comfortable person she'd met on that small island. The one she'd fallen in love with…and walked out on.

She stopped near a flight of stone steps leading to a heavy-looking front door, parking next to a pearl white limo whose engine was still running. Behind the wheel, the driver napped, his cap pulled down over his eyes. Trent, she knew, usually drove himself, and even when he didn't, he wouldn't be caught dead in a stretch limo. The additional car meant he had a guest.

Great timing. She shut off her car with trembling fingers and got out. For all the time it took her to mount them, the stairs might have been a hundred feet high. At the top, she lifted her hand to the bell—and then the door swung open. *Please be a maid,* she prayed, her eyes squeezed shut. *Or a butler.*

No such luck. Trent was there, still wearing the tailored suit he'd had on during the press conference in De Menzes Park, minus the jacket. On TV, he looked fantastic. It was only close up that she noticed how his tie brought out the melted toffee of his eyes. They held hers, showing less surprise than she'd expected, considering she'd turned up unannounced.

A surge of powerful emotion ripped through her, something sharp and bright. It was as if her dulled senses suddenly came alive again. Just being within two feet of this man could do that. It was scary. Her instinct for self-preservation yelled at her to run, but all she could do was look away, shield her eyes before he could read them. Before she was tempted to look into his to see what was there.

His mouth was relaxed and neutral, giving nothing away. "Hi."

"I got your fish," she said, which, as conversation starters went, was a little ridiculous.

He answered in all seriousness, "I couldn't bring the *wabine* home, of course. I left it with Anke."

"I got the, uh, necklace, too." Brilliant dialogue, coming from a writer.

"So I see: you're wearing it."

She forced herself not to cover it with her hands.

Trent filled her speechless moment by offering her his arm. "Come inside. I was just finishing up a business meeting. Then we can…talk."

The fabric of his shirt was rough under her fingers, and the skin and bone beneath like stone, but she knew it was just her mind playing tricks, her heightened awareness intensifying every sensation.

She would kill to learn more about him from observing his home, but as she followed him inside, only snatches of the decor came to her befuddled brain. Warmth and light, softly polished surfaces. There were lush plants in corners, and shelves laden with books. And a huge man filled the doorway to a spacious, formal sitting room. Enrique Palacio, Shanique's manager.

Dakota cursed silently. Enrique cursed out loud. "What the hell's going on?"

"I have a visitor," Trent informed him mildly.

Enrique gave her an ugly look. "We're in a meeting."

"Which is three minutes from being over," Trent responded shortly.

"I can wait outside," she began, but he led her into the room, using his body to shield her from the hate rays the other man was shooting at her. On the coffee table were spread a number of documents, and next to them, a bottle of fine bourbon and two half-filled glasses.

Trent indicated one of the heavy armchairs. "Sit, Dakota, this will only take a minute."

Enrique responded with such vehemence that spittle flew from his rubbery lips. "Are you out of your mind? Why don't you just hook up a live feed and beam this meeting out via the internet? You think losing her filthy little column makes her any less dangerous? She's an editor now, and new enough in the business to have something to prove." Enrique's shadow fell over the sheaf of papers on the desk, and as he yelled, his jowls wobbled, making her think briefly of Malcolm, the iguana. "Tell me you don't trust this woman to keep her trap shut?"

Dakota froze, a pain under her ribcage so sharp it was better not to inhale. Trent was standing over the table as well, and both men dwarfed her, intimidating her for differing reasons. His eyes sought hers. She wanted desperately to look away, but couldn't. Trust. The stumbling block upon which their fresh new love had fallen. He hadn't trusted her before, and there was no reason to think he would—

"Of course I do," he said, addressing himself to Enrique but rocking her world with the words.

She said a silent prayer of thanks that she was sitting down. Her body felt as heavy as a sack of grain.

Enrique snorted, wrapped a meaty fist around his glass and drained it. "That makes you a fool."

"That makes me a better judge of character than I thought," Trent said crisply. He sat before the pile of documents, seized a thick silver pen, and signed his name at the bottom of a page. He flipped through, initialing here and there, and then grimly handed it over to the other man, who hadn't bothered to take a seat.

Trent spoke again. "Dakota, Shanique and I are dissolving our contract. By…mutual agreement. It's effective immediately, but since she's still in rehab, we think it would be better if we wait until she's released before we make it public. It could be several months."

Enrique made a rude sound, and looked about to say something vile, but a hard look from Trent killed that idea. Instead, he shoved the documents into a large brown envelope, and clamped them to his chest. "Let it be known that I don't approve of this," he grunted.

"What, exactly? Dissolving a relationship that's no longer working, or discussing it in front of Dakota?"

"Both," the man snapped.

"Let me show you out, Enrique." Trent rose with a determination that couldn't be refused, and Dakota watched, her thoughts still spinning, as he led the man out. She listened as though from a great distance as the front door opened and closed, and a car engine retreated. Then, footsteps came her way.

She leaped to her feet, unwilling to remain at such a significant height disadvantage. Trent paused at the entrance to the room, rubbing his hands together thoughtfully, as if warming them. "Would you like a drink?"

She shook her head.

He stepped toward her, and when he was near, let his eyes run over her from top to toe. "You look good."

"Uh, you, too."

When he smiled, it was as if the colors she'd been starving for came back into her life. "Trent…"

He cupped her cheek, then ran a finger along the fine scar under her chin, the legacy of her fall at Rapture. "All healed?"

"What? Oh, yes." She didn't want him to distract her from what she needed to ask, so she persisted. "Why did you do that? You could have sent me to another room until you two settled your business."

He shook his head. "No need."

"You took a risk. I'm still media, remember, the scum of the—" He cut her off with a kiss that was so light and fast she wondered for a second if she'd imagined it. But the zing that rushed through her told her she certainly hadn't.

"You've proven yourself, even though you didn't have to. I was wrong to ask you to withhold the Shanique story. I'll always be ashamed of that. I made you choose between your professional integrity and me."

"I didn't hold on the story because you asked me, I did it because it was the right thing to do."

He shook his head regretfully. "You still lost your job."

"I got a new one," she reminded him, hating the idea of his guilt causing him pain.

One corner of his mouth curved upward. "All the same, it must have been hard. You were very brave."

Although his praise fell like rain on dry ground, she wouldn't allow herself to revel in it. "It doesn't mean I'll never step on anyone's toes. I'd be a lousy writer if I didn't. I make my living off other people's stories, and sometimes those stories aren't pretty."

His answer was soothing, determined. "We'll deal with that if it happens. We'll take the challenges as they come."

It was all sounding too good for her to believe. Something had to be wrong here. "We? What *we?* I haven't seen you in three months. You haven't called or sent a message—"

"I thought you hated me."

The pain on his face made her long to comfort him. "I could never hate you."

"You rushed out of Tobago without even giving me a chance to talk you into staying." He held his hands out, appealing to her for understanding. "You so desperately didn't want anything to do with me."

"If you thought that, why'd you send the fish?"

He chewed on his lower lip, frowning as if he had no idea. "It was lame, and stupid—" She tried to cut him off, but he went on. "I couldn't stand the loneliness. I was missing you every second of every day, and I wondered if there was any way to let you know how sorry I was...."

She was astounded. "You thought of me every day?"

His brows lifted, as if the question surprised him. Instead of answering, he held out his hand. After a second's hesitation, she took it. He led her through the house, stopping eventually at a large sliding door, and with a fluid movement, sent it skating sideways on its runners. He hit a switch, flooding the patio beyond with golden light.

Dakota gasped. The wooden decking was the pale blond of Tobago sand. String hammocks swung between pillars, and beyond, in the open, was a sunken pool, surrounded by rocks and ferns. Soft green floodlights glowed below the surface of the rippling water. It was as if a giant hand had torn Rapture's grotto loose, scooped it up, and transplanted it here, in Santa Amata, in Trent's massive backyard.

A row of dark-leafed saplings skirted the pool at its farthest end. They couldn't be, Dakota thought, but voiced the question anyway. "Tell me those aren't…"

"Orange trees," he confirmed. "Don't know how they'll survive in winter, but…"

She swung to look at him, tearing her eyes from the incredible setting before her. "Why'd you do this?"

The question seemed to puzzle him. "I don't know. I guess this is where we went off the rails. One minute, everything was perfect.…" He stopped, and she knew they were both thinking about what had happened that night in the green grotto, the intimacy they'd shared before…

"Then I mentioned Isaiah," she finished for him, "and ruined everything."

He hung his head. "I'm sorry. I overreacted. I had no right—"

She put her hand on his arm. "We both screwed up. We both said things at Rapture we'd like to take back, but we can't."

He grasped her and spun her to him. His expression was intense. "We don't need to take anything back. We just need to move on from here." He caught her up in his arms and brought his lips to hers. After all these months of longing, knowing something in her life was missing and there was no way she could fill that aching space, she gave up any idea of a battle, pressing against him, parting her lips.

He stopped to look down on her, happy relief shining in his eyes. "All the mistakes we made mean nothing.... What we can be to each other means everything."

Giddy from his kiss, she could hear her voice slur. "What can we be to each other?"

He smiled the kind of smile that had come so easily to him in Tobago. It made her breath catch. "Lovers. *Love*-ers. Two people who want to be together because they desire each other, have faith in each other, trust each other. *Love* each other."

Her fighting spirit wouldn't let her give in easily. "How do you know I..." She stopped. Once she said those words, she wouldn't be able to take them back. She realized she was blushing madly.

He knew he had her. His smile widened. "Go on."

She gasped out the rest in a gust. "...love you?"

"You told me."

"I did no such thing!"

"You wore this." His finger came up to stroke her jumbie bead necklace, then strayed to her collarbone, and then down the front of her scooped neckline to the tops of her breasts. After months of being untouched, they rose to meet his fingers.

"Matches my dress," she gasped, still knee-deep in denial.

"Huh." He was grinning, knowing she was only

throwing up barriers for the sake of it. "You told me in Tobago, in the grotto."

She frowned. She knew she'd never… "How?"

His mouth closed over hers again. "Like this."

A thunderstorm broke. She put her arms up around his head, pressing him to her, opening her mouth for his curious, probing tongue. *Trent,* a voice whispered inside her. *Trent, Trent…* "Kisses don't mean…" She tried to protest.

He cut her off. "I love you."

Oh, how she wanted to believe him! But it was impossible. Logic said it couldn't be. "We spent only four days together.…"

"I love you, anyway. And we're going to spend many more. More than you can count." His hands were on her hips, pressing her against his body, and she could feel nothing but welcoming warmth.

It seemed so easy. All she had to do was give up, give in, admit she loved him, and they could move on from there. So simple…and so hard. He waited, patiently, hands stroking her back in a rhythm that would have lulled her into sleep, if she weren't standing on the edge of a life-changing moment. He didn't try to press her or cajole, and for that she loved him even more.

"Trent…"

"Hm?"

"Trent…I…"

She felt laughter rumble through his chest. "There's no penalty for saying it, you know. You don't get sent back to 'start' or anything."

The beads around her neck were as warm as his touch. If they'd been proof enough for him, they were proof enough for her. She crumbled. "…love you."

The laughter deep inside him found its way out. She punched him on the shoulder. "What's so funny?"

"You say it like it's a death sentence, but it's not." He pressed kisses against her eyelids. "It's a promise of life. A promise of forever. Bygones will be bygones, and we can move on to something glorious."

She smiled back up at him. Glorious. She liked the sound of that. She discovered to her shock that she was airborne again, as he swept her up into his arms and carried her across his deck to one of the huge, swaying hammocks and set her down. Surely he wasn't—

He clambered in with her, and the contraption rocked wildly as he turned to press his body against hers. "Can this hold us?" she asked nervously.

"If it doesn't, at least we haven't got far to fall," he chuckled. Then his hands got very, very busy, pulling on the sash around her waist, popping the buttons on her dress and pushing it down. In the struggle to un-hook and remove her bra, they and their hammock al-most came to grief, but he mastered the maneuver and she was nearly naked under him. His hand closed over her breast, cupping it, and when he lowered his head to it she squeezed her eyes shut, anticipating the contact of tongue on nipple.

But instead, he pressed his lips against the inner curve of her breast, so he could feel the solidity of her ribs under his lips. She let out a groan of frustration. Her nipple wanted him, and it wanted him now! "What are you—"

"Shh." He didn't lift his head. "I can feel it."

"Feel what?"

"The beat. Your heart. I can feel it through your skin,

against my mouth." He turned his head and rested his ear against the same spot. "I can hear it, too."

The curiosity was killing her. The intimacy of the gesture even more. She curled her hand around his neck, holding him against her breast, enjoying the warmth of his breath against her bare skin.

"What can you hear?"

"Jazz."

She laughed at the unexpectedness of it. "Really?"

"Really." He lifted his head so that their eyes met and held. "It's in your heart. Mine, too. How could we not be meant for each other?"

She reached down to his belt buckle and undid it, struggling to yank it free while their hammock swayed crazily. "If you can hear my jazz, my love, and I can hear yours…" The zipper went down easily under her greedy fingers. "Then I have just one suggestion to make."

He lifted his hips, allowing her to free him of his trousers, and then watched with frank admiration as she wriggled out of her panties and threw them onto the deck. "What suggestion?"

"That you and I pick up the tempo."

They then put on a performance neither of them would ever forget.

* * * * *

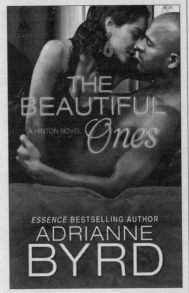

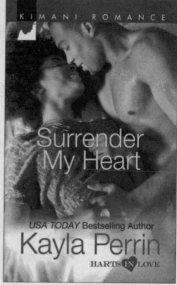

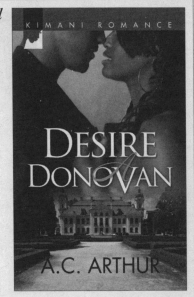

REQUEST YOUR FREE BOOKS!

2 FREE NOVELS
PLUS 2 FREE GIFTS!

KIMANI™
ROMANCE

Love's ultimate destination!

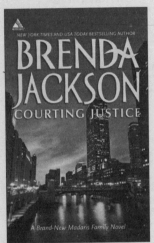